Del signo Libra en el zodiaco occidental y Caballo en el chino, IVÁN MONALISA OJEDA *nació en la Región de Los Lagos, sur de Chile. Estudió Artes Escénicas en la Facultad de Artes de la Universidad de Chile. Llegó a Nueva York un otoño de 1996, y desde entonces vive en esta ciudad.* Never, ever ever, coming down *es la traducción de* La misma nota, forever, *su primer libro.*

MARC BRUDZINSKI *vive en Nueva York y enseña Estudios Latinoamericanos y traducción en Purchase College (State University of New York).*

A Libra under the Western zodiac and a horse under the Chinese zodiac, **IVÁN MONALISA OJEDA** was born in Región de los Lagos, Southern Chile. He studied Scenic Arts at Universidad de Chile and she arrived to New York City on an autumn day in 1996. She has lived in the city since then. *Never, Ever Ever, Coming Down* (originally in Spanish *La misma nota, forever*) is her first book.

MARC BRUDZINSKI lives in New York City, and teaches Latin American Studies and translation at Purchase College (State University of New York).

LEGIBILITIES 2
FICTION / NARRATIVA

Iván Monalisa Ojeda

NEVER, EVER EVER, COMING DOWN

edición bilingüe / bilingual edition
translated by Marc Brudzinski

SANGRÍA

© Iván Monalisa Ojeda
ISBN: 978-956-8681-44-9
Original title: *La misma nota, forever* (Sangría Editora, 2014)

© translation and note, Marc Brudzinski

© cover photography, Camilo Fuentealba

© 2016, Sangría Legibilities Inc
1443 Dean Street, Apartment 2
Brooklyn, NY 11213, USA
info@sangriaeditora.com / www.sangriaeditora.com

Sangría Legibilities aims to create new models to issue discourses, texts, and literatures that are alive in the United States. By consolidating multilingualism in literature and other socially relevant texts and media, we offer a commitment to cultural openness, and we extend a social contract from the emergent languages of the Americas to the mainstream communities in the United States.

Editors: Carlos Labbé, Mónica Ríos,
        Carolina Alonso Bejarano, Peter Quach.
Layout design: Carlos Labbé.
Cover design: Peter Quach.

Printed in the United States of America.

CONTENTS

La gata siamesa

La barra está llena de monitores de televisión que muestran películas pornográficas, hombres con hombres que no parecen hombres. Son hombres con silicón, con implantes de agua salina. Hombres que han tomado hormonas. En cambio yo soy una travesti. Algo de origen más antiguo, casi mitológico. Y así, sintiéndome especial, bajo las escaleras para encontrarme con Isaac. Y ahí aparece él. Me acerco muy coqueta, preguntándole cómo le va. Él me dice que más o menos. Yo le pregunto por qué. Me dice lo que ya sé. Que ya está cansado de tanta medicina. De tantos años con ese cáncer que no desaparece. Yo para subirle el ánimo le digo que no se ve como una persona enferma. Que es bien parecido, de cabello castaño y ojos claros, que tiene un buen trabajo, un regio departamento y una gata siamesa muy bonita que se llama Mimí. Me mira asombrado. Cómo puedo saber tanto de él. Y entonces tengo que recordarle que ya nos hemos ido muchas veces juntos. Que siempre conversamos. Que siempre hemos tenido buen sexo. Y que además me paga muy

The Siamese Cat

The bar is full of monitors showing porno movies, men with men that don't look like men. They are men with silicone implants, with saline implants. Men who have taken hormones. Me, however, I'm a travesti. Something with more ancient, almost mythological origins. So that's how I go down the stairs, feeling special, down to meet up with Isaac. And there he is. I approach him flirtatiously, asking him how he's doing. He gives me an answer I already knew. How he's tired of taking so many meds. Of so many years with this cancer that won't go away. To cheer him up I tell him he doesn't look like someone who's sick. That he's good-looking, chestnut-brown hair and light eyes, that he has a good job, an awesome apartment and a pretty Siamese cat named Mimi. He looks at me, surprised. How could I know so much about him? That's when I have to remind him that we've already been together several times. That we always talk. That we've always had good sex. And that he pays me well, too. He laughs and, smiles

bien. Se ríe y con su sonrisa me dice que por supuesto. Y que también soy bella, muy bella, bella como tantas otras que caminan por esta barra buscando clientela con sus carteras hambrientas como la mía. Le pregunto si sigue al pie de la letra el tratamiento médico. Me dice que sí, mientras me invita un blow de cocaína. Yo, que me había propuesto no hacer drogas esta noche, acepto. Nos quedamos en silencio. Me ofrece un trago. Yo pido un vodka and cranberry juice. Me pongo de pie y me voy a otro rincón de la barra. Ese pase de coca me ha dejado para adentro, pensando en nada. Veo a Isaac que habla con una y con otra. Bebe y se echa cocaína. Yo quiero otro jale. Me acerco y se lo pido. Me lo da. Me ofrece otro vodka and cranberry juice. Le toco el rostro. Es una cara de niño: dulce, pálido y de ojos transparentemente azules. Le doy un beso en el cuello. A lo vampire. Él me acaricia las piernas. Le muerdo la oreja y susurrando le pregunto por mi propina. Me da cincuenta dólares. Me pongo de pie. Quiero dejarlo a solas por un momento. Ya sé que esta noche él será mi one night stand plus money.

Caminando por ahí me encuentro con Mirella, una loca mexicana. Comentamos que la situación no está buena. Que hay que llegar más temprano para hacer algún dinero. Claro. The early bird gets the early worm. Me pide un sorbo de mi trago, se lo bebe todo en un santiamén. Voy donde la bartender y le pido

«of course.» And that I too am beautiful, very beautiful, beautiful just like so many other girls walking through this bar looking for clients, their wallets as hungry as mine. I ask him if he follows his doctor's orders to the letter. He says he does, and invites me to do some blow. Although I had resolved not to do any drugs tonight, I accept. We stand there for a minute in silence. He offers to buy me a drink. I order a vodka and cranberry juice. I stand up and go to another corner of the bar. That snort of coke took me inside myself, where I stay, thinking of nothing. I see Isaac talking with this girl, then with that girl. He's drinking and sniffing coke. I want another jale so I go up to him and ask for one. He gives it to me. Then he offers me another vodka and cranberry juice. I touch his face. He has a babyface: sweet, pale, with eyes so blue they're almost clear. I give him a kiss on the neck. Like a vampire. He caresses my legs. I bite his ear and whisper for my tip. He gives me fifty dollars. I stand up. I want to leave him by himself for a moment. I know that tonight he will be my one-night stand plus money.

While I'm walking around I run into Mirella, a Mexican loca. We talk about how business is not good. About how you need to get here early if you want to make any money. Claro. The early bird gets the worm. She asks for a sip of my drink and before

uno gratis. *Me da el correspondiente vodka and cranberry juice otra vez. Como ella es filipina le digo:*

—Salamat!

Siento las narices picándome. Prendo un cigarrillo, una loca me pide una fumada. Le digo que sí, pero sólo una, pues es el último que me queda. Lo agarra y se va. Decido volver donde Isaac. Lo encuentro sentado en el mismo lugar. Solo. Seguramente ya le sacaron todo el dinero. Entre la oscuridad de la barra me hace gestos con las manos para que me acerque. Cuando estoy a su lado veo sus ojos tan abiertos que parece que se le van a salir de las cuencas. Me cuenta que se le acabó la coca. Le digo que compre más. Me responde que también se le acabó el dinero. Le propongo que compremos una bolsa con el mío. Que de ahí nos vayamos juntos a su casa. Que pase a un cajero automático y que me devuelva el dinero de la droga, sin contar lo que me debe pagar por mis servicios. Así lo hacemos. Tomamos un taxi y cruzando el Williamsburg Bridge llegamos a su departamento en Brooklyn. Una vez adentro le pido que no encienda las luces. Que con la luz de la calle que entra por los ventanales es más que suficiente. Su gata Mimí está en un rincón, inmóvil como una pequeña estatua egipcia.

Nos vamos a su dormitorio. Me desnudo. Lo desnudo. Pongo algo de coca en la cabeza de mi verga erecta. Isaac lo succiona hasta el cansancio. Me vengo

I can say no, she drinks it all up. I go over to the Filipina bartender and ask for a free drink. She gives me another vodka and cranberry juice. I tell her «Salamat!» in honor of her heritage.

My nostrils are itchy. I light up, a loca asks for a drag off my cigarette. I say OK, but just one, because it's my last. She grabs it and leaves. I decide to go back to Isaac. I find him sitting in the same place. Alone. They must have already taken all his money. Through the darkness of the bar he motions for me to come closer. When I am next to him I see his eyes are open so wide that they seem like they might pop out of their sockets. He tells me that he's out of coke. I tell him to buy some more. He tells me that he's also out of money. I suggest we buy a bag with my money. And that from there we should go back to his place. That he can hit an ATM and give me back the money for the drugs, plus the money for my services. So that's what we do. We take a taxi over the Williamsburg Bridge to his Brooklyn apartment. Once inside, I ask him not to turn the lights on. The light coming in through the tall windows is more than enough. His cat Mimi is over in a corner, motionless like a little Egyptian statue.

We go to his bedroom. I take my clothes off. I take his clothes off. I put a little coke on my erect cock. Isaac sucks it off with all his energy. I come

dentro de su boca. Nos relajamos por varios segundos. Me visto mientras él llama un taxi que me regresará a Manhattan.

Antes de despedirnos, antes de abrir la puerta, Isaac prende las luces del departamento. Veo claramente a su gata Mimí que reposa en sus brazos. Veo claramente el amplio departamento. Veo claramente la cara de Isaac. Veo claramente que todo tiene el color de las cenizas.

in his mouth. We relax for a few seconds. I get dressed while he calls for a taxi to take me back to Manhattan.

Before we say goodbye, before opening the door, Isaac turns the lights on. I see clearly his cat Mimi resting in his arms. I see the whole huge apartment clearly. I see Isaac's face clearly. I see clearly that everything has the color of ashes.

El fan club de la Turner

Escribo entre penumbras. El studio de la Manuel se alumbra con la pantalla de un televisor encendido, sin volumen. Una luz violeta más una cortina de tules dividen el espacio en dos, y hacen que el dueño de casa, la Manuel, y el invitado de ocasión se vean desde lejos con los bordes de sus cuerpos iluminados. Se acarician. Me invitan a participar. Yo no quiero. El crystal me tiene sin ganas de sexo; una cosa extraña, pues a todo el mundo le da con eso de meterse con uno y con otro, y con el que venga. Hasta que se termina en una orgía. Manuel me dice:

–Monalisa, ya no nos echemos mas Tina, que si no nos vamos directo al emergency room.

Crystal meth, también conocida como Tina. Así que cuando hablamos para conseguirla nos decimos:

–Oye loquita, ¿cómo estás para escuchar el último CD de la Tina Turner?

–Me parece buena idea. A ver si consigues varios CD, así podemos revenderlos a algunos fanáticos.

–Claro. Yo conozco un fan club de la Tina Turner que es súper numeroso. ¡Numerosísimo!

La Turner's Fan Club

I'm writing in the shadows. La Manuel's studio is lit by the screen of a TV set, no volume. A violet light plus a tulle curtain divide the space into two, and let you see la Manuel, and his guest for the night, from afar –– the edges of their bodies lit up. They caress each other. They invite me to join in. I don't want to. Crystal leaves me without a sex drive; a strange thing, since it makes everyone else want to get with each other, whoever's around. Until you end up in an orgy.

Manuel tells me, «Monalisa, we can't take any more Tina. If we do we'll wind up in the emergency room.»

Crystal meth, also known as Tina. So when we're talking about getting some, we say, «Oye loquita, how would you like to listen to Tina Turner's latest CD?»

«Sounds like a good idea. Maybe you could get a bunch of CD's. Then we could sell them to her fans.»

«Claro. I know one of Tina Turner's fan clubs that has a lot of members. A lot.»

El invitado esta noche es un conocido de la Ma-
nuel, recién llegado de Pittsburgh. Un trip en bus de
casi cuatro horas para volverse loquito en Nueva York.
Un tipo del que ni siquiera sé su nombre. Es blanco,
yo diría que italiano. Entre treinta y treinticinco años.
En una escala de uno a diez yo le daría un siete. De
pronto lo miro y me hace señas para que vaya a la
cama junto a él. Voy y le agarro el miembro que esta
embadurnado en lubricante. Es una verga como de
ocho pulgadas. Sí, en verdad es un trozo grande. Él
no es feo. Pero es que no sé. Que tenga el cabello con
highlights en la onda metrosexual –porque todos los
gays no son metrosexuales, ni todos los metrosexuales
son gays–, pues eso, chulita, a mí no me calienta. Es
como ver a una amiga más, con esa que chismoseas y
te vas por ahí de copas a conversar de las desgracias
mutuas. Porque en lo que se refiere a mí prefiero un
construction worker o un truck driver. Un irlandés de
aquellos que se van a los bares a beber por horas, y que
nunca se van al suelo por más borrachos que estén.
Igual le pregunto al invitado de Pittsburgh:
–Do you like to get fuck with a dildo?
Me mira.
–Yes, but first I have to get a shower.
Y yo vuelvo a sentarme aquí, en la otra esquina del
studio, en esta mesita negra muy chic que la Manuel se
encontró en la calle. Porque debo aclarar que la Manuel

Tonight's special guest is an acquaintance of la Manuel, and he's recently in from Pittsburgh. A bus trip of almost four hours to come to New York and get crazy. A guy whose name I don't even know. He's white, I would say probably Italian. Between thirty and thirty-five. On a scale of one to ten I'd give him a seven. I look over at him and he motions for me to come get in bed with him. I go and grab his penis, which is covered in lube. It's like eight inches. That's right –– a very big piece. He's not ugly. But I just don't know. For him to have highlights in his hair, metrosexual-style –– because all gays are not metrosexual and all metrosexuals are not gay –– it just doesn't make me horny, chulita. It's like being with another girl, one of your good girlfriends you gossip with and go out for drinks with and talk about your collective sorrows. Because as far as I'm concerned I'd much rather have a construction worker or a truck driver. One of those Irish guys who go to the bars and drink for hours, and never fall off their stool no matter how drunk they get.

I ask the guest from Pittsburgh anyway, «Do you like to get fucked with a dildo?»

He looks at me. «Yes, but first I have to take a shower.»

And so I sit down back over here, in the other corner of the studio, at the chic little black table that la Manuel found in the street. I should probably mention that

tiene muy buen gusto en lo que a decoración se refiere. Y
esta otra, mi amiga a la que voy a empezar a llamar miss
Tina, esta miss Tina me tiene escribiendo a lo acelerado.
Escribo y escribo, y de pronto me detengo. Me pongo de
pie, bajo a la tienda. Bajo las escaleras de este building
viejo donde vive la Manuel, en la Octava Avenida entre
las calles Quince y Catorce. Chelsea neighborhood. En
la esquina compro dos galones de agua y un sobre de
Tylenol PM para lo que se pudiera presentar. Aunque,
pensándolo bien, esto de las píldoras fue un gasto inne-
cesario. La Manuel tiene tal cantidad de pastillas, desde
Xanax hasta morfina, pasando por Viagra y Ambien,
que lo de ella es una verdadera farmacia. Y ahí estaba
yo de compras bien seguro de mí mismo, a pesar de que
sabía que todo el mundo me estaba mirando; en especial
cuando entré a comprar el sancocho en La Taza de Oro.

–Es que la Tina se ve, Monalisa –me había dicho la
Manuel–. Se ve en los ojos. Las pupilas se te agrandan
como platillos.

Vuelvo al studio. Dejo mis compras en el suelo. Abro
un galón de agua. Bebo como si fuera la última coca
cola del desierto y comienzo a escribir de nuevo.

–¡Monalisa, ven! –grita la Manuel.

Y yo me acerco a la cama donde esta con el invitado de Pittsburgh.

–¿Por qué no vas a recoger un delivery de Tina?
–me dice la muy descarada.

la Manuel has very good taste when it comes to home decor. And my other good girlfriend, the one I'm going to call Miss Tina, well this Miss Tina has me writing, at breakneck speed. I write and write, and suddenly I stop. I get up to go down to the store. I go down the staircase of this old building la Manuel's living in, on Eighth Avenue between 15th and 14th. Chelsea. On the corner I buy two gallons of water and a packet of Tylenol PM to be prepared for whatever. Although, now that I think about it, those pills were a waste of money. La Manuel has such a supply of pills, from Xanax to morphine, not to mention the Viagra and the Ambien, that she's basically a one-man pharmacy. So there I was, completely sure of myself, even though I could tell everyone was looking at me; especially when I went in to buy a bowl of sancocho at La Taza de Oro.

«You can just tell when someone's on Tina, Monalisa,» la Manuel had told me. «You can see it in the eyes. Your pupils get as big as saucers.»

I go back up to the studio. I leave my purchases on the floor. I drink as if I were drinking the last Coca Cola in the desert and I start writing again.

«Monalisa, come here!» shouts la Manuel.

So I go over to the bed where he's lying with the guest from Pittsburgh.

«Why don't you go pick up a *delivery* of Tina,» la Manuel asks me, la muy descarada.

Y pienso: qué se cree ella. Que no ve que estoy es-
cribiendo. Que mi escritura no se puede interrumpir
así como así. Pues le alego:

–¡No!

Luego vuelvo a pensarlo:

–¡Sí!

Pero será a cambio de algunas exigencias. Y nue-
vamente vuelvo a pensarlo. Voy o no voy. Pienso. No,
no pienso. Estoy high. Y estoy paranoico. Nueva York
está en alerta naranja, alerta de que puede haber al-
gún ataque terrorista. Se ve que anda mucho under-
cover por ahí. Se esperan más atentados en la ciudad,
como si nadie que viva en Nueva York no lo supiera.
Cuando quede la catástrofe en el subway durante el
rush hour. O cuando lancen alguna bomba viral peor
que el VIH y Nueva York quede aislado. O algo conge-
lante, en la onda Day After Tomorrow. No, no quiero
salir. De pronto el invitado de Pittsburgh se viste y se
va. Qué tiene que hacer.

La Manuel me dice:

–Va a volver.

Y de inmediato salta de la cama a la mesita que se
ha convertido en mi escritorio.

–Oye Monalisa, este tipo vuelve ahora. Así que si-
gue la corriente en todo lo que te diga.

–Qué quieres decir.

–Pues que hay que sacarle dinero, chica.

And I think, who does she think she is. Can't she see I'm writing. You know my writing can't be interrupted just like that.

So I tell him «No!»

Then I think about it some more. «Yes!»

But it will be in exchange for some demands. And then I think again. Should I go or not. I think. No, I don't think. I'm high. And I'm paranoid. New York is on orange alert, meaning there could be a terrorist attack. You can tell there are a lot of undercover cops around. They're expecting more terrorist attempts, as if anyone who lives in New York didn't already know that. Whenever they manage to carry out the catastrophe in the subway system during rush hour. Or when they set off a virus worse than HIV and New York goes into quarantine. Or a freeze-over like in Day After Tomorrow. No, I don't want to go out. Suddenly the guest from Pittsburgh gets dressed and leaves. What does he think he has to do?

La Manuel tells me, «He's coming back.»

And immediately he jumps from the bed to the little table I turned into my writing desk.

«Oye, Monalisa. This guy will come back. So just go with the flow, whatever I tell you to do.»

«What do you mean.»

«We need to get some money out of him, chica.»

Acordamos con la Manuel no meternos más Tina, y dormirnos a la medianoche. Yo llevo treintidós horas sin hacerlo y la Manuel algo más de dos días. Me dice que me va a dar una píldora de Xanax; bueno, la mitad, pues una entera es muy peligroso. Nos ponemos a limpiar el studio. Llega el momento de limpiar la alfombra, pero no estoy en la onda de pasar la aspiradora. Así que la Manuel me dice:

–Mira chica, la que va a dormir en el suelo esta noche eres tú. Así que si quieres dormir en la mugre, ¡no limpies ni pinga!

Y ahí me quede yo. Leída y entinada. Le estaba sacando la vuelta a la limpieza. Eso sí debo decir que pelé unos mangos y corté en trocitos varios strawberries, dejándolos hermosamente decorados en un plato para que la Manuel se las comiera cuando estuviera de antojo. Pero la Manuel, que es muy buena para la leída, agrega:

–Seguro que lo hiciste para comértelo más tarde.

Qué mal pensada y qué mal agradecida.

Tal como él lo había previsto, el invitado de Pittsburgh regresó. Apenas entra al studio se empieza a desvestir. Saca una bolsa de Tina. La vacía en un billete de veinte dólares para molerla. La Manuel toma el billete estirado y me ofrece. La miro: ¿no te acuerdas en lo habíamos quedado? ¿No más Tina y dormirnos a la medianoche? Y él me mira de vuelta: ¿y para qué

La Manuel and I agreed not to take any more Tina, and to get to bed by midnight. I haven't slept in thirty-two hours, and la Manuel hasn't slept in over two days. He tells me he's going to give me a Xanax; well, a half a Xanax because a whole one can be dangerous. We start cleaning the studio. Time comes to clean the rug, but I don't feel like vacuuming.

So la Manuel tells me, «Look girl, if anyone's sleeping on the floor tonight it's you. So if you don't mind sleeping in all this grime, you don't have to clean shit!»

So there I go. Read up and down and all tina'd out. I was avoiding doing the cleaning. I will say that I peeled a few mangoes and chopped up some strawberries, leaving them beautifully laid out on a plate for la Manuel to eat when she got a craving.

But la Manuel, who always was good at reading, adds, «I'm sure you did this so you could eat them later yourself.»

How cynical of her. How ungrateful.

Just as la Manuel had said, the guest from Pittsburgh came back. As soon as he gets inside the studio he starts to undress. He takes out a bag of Tina. He empties it out onto a twenty-dollar bill to grind it up. La Manuel takes out a smoothed-out bill and offers it to me. I look at her: don't you remember what we agreed on? No more Tina and going to sleep at midnight? He

me haces caso, que no ves que el embale me hace decir tonterías? Pero bueno. Me doy dos jales. Dos jales bien fuertes. El televisor siempre ha estado encendido, pero sin volumen. Nos ponemos a ver el último episodio de American Idol, un fast food singer. No fish, no meat. Igual nunca supimos cómo cantaban. Mientras el invitado de Pittsburgh se sobaba la verga, le pregunto qué siente cuando está en Tina.

–I feel horny –me responde.

La Manuel se levanta de la cama y se sienta junto a mí. Ahora yo me paso de la mesita negra a la cama. Me estiro y me trato de relajar. Estoy al lado del invitado de Pittsburgh. De pronto, como corresponde a su carácter celoso y dominante, la Manuel se pone histérica. Abre aun más esos ojos azules que cautivan a todo el mundo, menos a mí. El invitado de Pittsburgh roza con sus pies los míos. Con sus piernas, mi espalda. Y yo no estoy ni ahí. El tipo este no me gusta. Lo veo como a una loca más. Una amiga. Y yo no soy lesbiana: me gustan los hombres, y que se vean bien hombres. La Manuel sigue en su histeria. Sin saber que yo nada de nada con el invitado de Pittsburgh, vocifera:

–Monalisa, ¡la nota de Tina te puso en la onda agresiva!

Y yo, para nada. De la más nice, de lo más inspirada, de lo más artística. Ella no puede con mi attitude.

26

looks back at me: so now is when you start listening to me? Just when the drugs make me say stupid things? Whatever. I do two bumps. Two strong bumps. The TV has been on, but with no sound. We start to watch the finale of American Idol. A fast-food singer –– no fish, no meat. We never really heard how they were singing, anyway. While the guest from Pittsburgh was rubbing on his dick, I ask him how he feels when he's on Tina.

«I feel horny,» he answers me.

La Manuel gets up from bed and sits down next to me. Now I go from the little black table to the bed. I stretch out and try to relax. I'm next to the guest from Pittsburgh. Suddenly, as you might expect given her jealous and domineering nature, la Manuel gets hysterical. She opens those blue eyes that captivate everyone but me even wider. The guest from Pittsburgh strokes my feet with his. And my back with his legs. I'm not really there anymore. The guy doesn't do it for me. I see him as just another good girlfriend. I'm no lesbian: I like men, and I mean men who look like men. La Manuel goes on with her hysteria.

Not knowing I want nothing to do with the guest from Pittsburgh, she shouts, «Monalisa, that Tina has made you get all aggressive!»

But I pay her no mind. I'm keeping it all nice. So inspired, so artistic. She can't stand my attitude. So she

Así que salta de la mesita a la cama, se instala entre mí y el invitado de Pittsburgh. Me levanto y voy al baño. Al salir me dirijo a la mesita y sigo escribiendo. Me dicen que salgamos por ahí a caminar. Yo pienso en que tengo que escribir y luego descansar. Que llevo muchas horas despierto.

–No voy –les replico.

Ellos se visten y antes de que salgan les digo:

–Girls, have fun!

Y ahí sigo yo. High. Escribiendo. Bebiendo mucha agua. Listo para empezar con el segundo galón. Mucha, mucha agua para limpiar este cuerpo intoxicado. Sigo escribiendo, mientras afuera la ciudad sigue su curso.

jumps from the little table to the bed, gets in between me and the guest from Pittsburgh. I get up and go to the bathroom. When I come out I go right to the little table and get back to my writing. They say we should go out and walk around. I think about how I have to write and then rest later. About how many hours I've been up.

«I'm not going,» I tell them.

They get dressed and as they're on their way out I tell them, «Girls, have fun!»

And so I go on. High. Writing. Drinking a lot of water. Ready to start on the second gallon. Lots and lots of water to clean out this intoxicated body. I keep writing while, outside, the city follows its course.

El nene ese le enseñó a pelear

Liz salió de la cárcel. Estuvo en Rikers Island por algo más de tres años. Había asaltado un grocery, una noche en que el mexicano que ahí cuidaba andaba medio despistado. La loca vació la caja registradora. Se embolsó como cuatro mil dólares. La policía no se tomó ni un mes en agarrarla. Bastó con revisar las huellas digitales dejadas en el campo de acción para que supieran a quién tenían que buscar. Y es que Liz tenía record, y uno de no pocas páginas; nada de delitos violentos, sólo robo y prostitución. No en vano era una legendary del Hell's Kitchen neighborhood. Cuando la policía fue a buscarla, la que abrió la puerta fue su mamá. Y ésta, cuando vio de quiénes se trataba, y como ya conocía las costumbres de su hija, sin decir palabra los dejó pasar. A Liz la encontraron en el patio de atrás, quizás todavía en la nota que le había dado el último pipazo de crack. Tenía para ese entonces treinta y siete años. Salió hace un par de semanas de Las Rokas. Tiene ya cuarenta y volvió otra vez a casa de su mamá.

That Boy Taught Her How to Fight

Liz got out of jail. She was on Rikers Island for a little over three years. She had held up a grocery, one night that the Mexican behind the counter was a little distracted. The girl emptied out the cash register. She pocketed like four thousand dollars. The police didn't even take a week to nab her. All they had to do was analyze the fingerprints left at the scene to know who they had to look for. Because Liz had a record, and more than a few pages long; no violent crimes, just robbery and prostitution. Not for nothing she was una legendary in Hell's Kitchen. When the police went to look for her, the one to open the door was her mother -- who, when she saw who it was, and since she knew her daughter's habits, let them in without saying a word. They found Liz out back, possibly still high from her last hit on the crack pipe. She was about thirty-seven at that time. She got out of Las Rokas a few weeks ago. Now she's forty and went back to her mom's house.

Nos la encontramos la otra noche. Yo caminaba con Silvia. La acompañamos a su casa. Con Silvia nos íbamos fumando un pito de marihuana. Liz no fumó. Dice que ya es hora de dejar las drogas. Dice que lo suyo es el crack y la heroína. Que eso es lo que a ella la tienta. Pero aun así el humo de la yerba la puede volver loca. Lo que fumábamos con Silvia, mientras caminábamos en dirección al río, era exotic weed, una especie bien fuerte de high drug. Ahora todo el mundo sólo fuma high drug. Yo no lo podía creer, ¿que Liz no quisiera fumar con nosotras? Pero sí, efectivamente no fumó. Silvia decía que ojalá le dure esa nota de estar clean por un buen tiempo, para despejar la mente. Le comenté que por lo menos estaba tratando, pero ya sabemos que no es fácil dejar las drogas así como así. En especial si vienes saliendo de la cárcel y dejas a tu amorcito allá dentro. Liz dice que el nene ese es bellísimo. Que aún le quedan como cinco años en Las Rokas. Que está preso por asesinato. Mató a una pareja, a un matrimonio, para ser más exactos. Pero como el crimen lo había cometido siendo menor de edad, la sentencia no fue tan severa. Y por eso sale como en cinco años más. Liz dice que no le tiene miedo. Que el nene ése la respeta. Que en el fondo es un buen muchacho. Que él tampoco se arrepentía de lo que había hecho. Que los mató porque lo habían traicionado. Que los mató delante de los niños.

We ran into her the other night. I was walking with Silvia. We walked her home. Silvia and I were smoking a joint as we walked. Liz didn't have any. She said it's time to lay off the drugs. She says her thing is crack and heroine, that's what she can't stay away from. But even without smoking any herself, the second-hand smoke can drive her crazy. What Silvia and I were smoking as we walked towards the river, was «exotic weed,» a really strong kind of high drug. Now everybody only smokes high drugs. I couldn't even believe it -- Liz didn't want to smoke with us? But no, she didn't. Silvia said hopefully this high from being clean lasts her for a while, to clear her head. I told her that at least she was trying, but we know that it's not so easy to kick the drugs just like that. Especially if you're just out of jail and you left your boyfriend inside. Liz tells us how beautiful this boy is. How he has like five years left in Las Rokas. How he's in for murder. He killed a couple, a married couple to be exact. But since he had committed the crime while he was a minor, the sentence wasn't that harsh. That's why he's out in five more years. Liz tells us how she's not scared of him. How this boy respects her. How deep down he's a good kid. How he did not regret what he did. How he killed them because they'd betrayed him. How he killed them in front of their kids.

Liz dice que lo va a esperar por estos cinco años que aún le quedan. A Liz se le ve fuerte y saludable. Dice que el nene le enseñó a pelear. Y eso que ella ya sabía pelear. Pero allá dentro sí que una tenía que saber cómo defenderse y hacerse respetar. En especial si eres una loca. Claro, podrías irte a Homo House. Pero no. A Liz le gusta estar con los hombres. Ser la reina del lugar. Así que saber defenderse era una necesidad. Dice que su novio será un asesino y todo, pero que a ella le hizo estar bien con él allá adentro. Que le quitó la frustración y todo eso de estar encerrada. Dormían en el mismo dormitorio, sus camas no estaban tan separadas una de la otra. Que cuando apagaban las luces ella se pasaba donde él. Y ahí en esa oscuridad, vigilando que el guardia no se apareciera, se unían con lujuria reprimida para no hacer ruido en ese dormitorio de sesenticuatro camas. Había que hacerlo rápido. No había tiempo para tanto besuqueo. Se trataba de zingar, de chichar, de descargarse, de venirse rápido, lo más rápido que se pudiera, que si los pillaban iban a la celda de castigo por un mes. La ducha, sólo dos veces a la semana, y no más al comedor a tragar esos platos sin sabor con los demás; nada de gimnasio y olvídate de la televisión. Por eso cuando ellos están juntos en esa oscuridad, y el guardia al otro lado de ese gran dormitorio, había que hacerlo rápido, bien rápido.

Liz says that she'll wait for him for these five years he has left. Liz looks strong and healthy. She says that this boy taught her how to fight. Not that she didn't know before. But in there you really needed to know how to defend yourself and get respect. Especially if you are a loca. Sure, you could go to Homo House. But no. Liz likes to be with the men. To be the queen of the whole place. So self-defense was a necessity. She says that her boyfriend may be a murderer and all, but it was good to be with him in there. It took away the frustration and all that from being locked up. They slept in the same room, their beds weren't that far apart. When they shut off the lights, she snuck over to him. And there in the dark, making sure that the guard didn't show up, they got together with repressed lust so as not to make noise in that room with sixty-four beds. They had to do it quickly. There wasn't time for making out. It was all about screwing, doing the nasty, letting off steam, coming fast, as fast as they could, because if they got caught it was off to solitary for a month. Showers only twice a week, and no more going to the mess hall with everyone to scarf down those bland meals; no gym and just forget about TV. So when they were together in the dark, and the guard on the other side of that big bedroom, they had to do it quick, real quick.

Seguimos caminando por el West Side. Ya había-
mos pasado como hace dos cuadras la casa de Liz.
Estábamos sentadas en una banqueta cerca del río. Al
frente se veía New Jersey. Ya era de noche. Una brisa
de verano propia de esta ciudad isla nos hizo quedar-
nos en silencio por unos segundos. Liz nos cuenta que
los días allá adentro se suceden a tiempo de compás.
Que la lluvia, el sol, el viento, la nieve parecen fenó-
menos cinematográficos a través de esos barrotes. No
poder hacer muñecos de nieve era lo que más frustra-
ba a Liz. Dice que se va a poner las pilas. Que va a
poner en orden todos sus papeles, que va a conseguir
el SSI, food stamps y todo eso. Que la ciudad le puede
pagar hasta la renta de un departamento. Es cosa de
que lo haga bien; con astucia, le dice Silvia. Que se
puede declarar demente. Que vaya a varias sesiones
con el siquiatra, que haga bastante drama, en la onda
de que se quiere suicidar, de que no sabe si es hombre
o mujer, de que siente que la gente la rechaza, hasta
que convenza al doctor de que está inhabilitada para
trabajar, y que por lo tanto aplica a ayuda guberna-
mental. Y para ponerse a hacer todo aquello debe es-
tar con la mente clara. Y ella está tratando, sí. Al me-
nos está tratando. Yo le doy ánimos. Le digo que para
ella es fácil, porque es puertorriqueña. Y se ve que Liz
quiere hacer las cosas bien. Vive con su mamá y ahí
no le hace falta nada.

We went on walking down the West Side. We were already two blocks past Liz's house. We were sitting on a bench near the river. Across the way you could see New Jersey. It was night time already. A summer breeze, the kind you only get on this island city, blew over us as we sat in silence for a few seconds. Liz tells us that the days on the inside follow one after another according to their own rhythm. The rain, sun, wind, and snow seem like cinematographic effects in a movie, through those bars. The thing that frustrated Liz the most was not being able to make snowmen. She talks about how she's really going to get everything together now. How she's going to get her papers in order, how she's going to get SSI, food stamps and all that. How the city could pay for even the rent on her own apartment. You just gotta do it right; gotta be clever about it, Silvia tells her. She could get them to declare her mentally ill. Just go to a couple of sessions with a shrink, make a scene, talk about how she wants to kill herself, how she doesn't know if she's a man or a woman, how people reject her, until she convinces the doctor that she's unfit for work, and therefore in need of government assistance. And before she starts in on all this, she needs to have a clear head. And she's trying, yes she is. At least she's trying. I encourage her. I tell her it's going to be easy for her, because she's Puerto Rican. And you can tell Liz wants to do things right. She lives with her mother and she's not wanting for anything there.

Liz estará pronto de cumpleaños. Dijo que iba a hacer una fiesta con una gran comelata. Y al saber que nosotras seríamos las primeras invitadas en probar los tamales, como siempre andamos con hambre, nos pusimos a saltar entre carcajadas.

It'll be Liz's birthday soon. She said she's going to have a party, with a big comelata. When she told us we'd be the first guests to taste the tamales, because we were always saying we were hungry, we busted out laughing.

El chico de al lado

Ni supe cuándo llegó a vivir al lado.

Es domingo y me levanto para ir al baño. La puerta está laqueada. Se escucha que alguien está tomando una ducha. Espero no más de tres minutos y, cuando estoy ready para devolverme, se abre la puerta. Frente a mí, un muchacho dominicano joven, grande, guapo y con cara de chico malo. Le evito la mirada y le digo Excuse me, mientras entro a darme una ducha. Lo hago y vuelvo a mi cuarto.

Anoche estuvo buena la barra. Me hice mis chavos. Llamo al Malecón para pedir un delivery de carne asada con moro negro, flan y una materva con mucho hielo. Es domingo y aún no quiero salir a la calle. Maybe later. Mientras esperaba por la comida, sentí cómo el recién llegado salía de su cuarto, ponía llave y pasaba cerca del mío con paso fuerte. Un chico seguro. Llega la comida. Me la como. Más bien me la trago. No puedo echarme en la cama, que si no me da una hinchazón de aquéllas. Salgo a la calle a tomarme un café. Bajando las escaleras del segundo piso me cruzo

The Boy from Next Door

I must not have noticed when he moved in next door.

It's Sunday and I get up to go to the bathroom. The door is locked. You can hear someone is taking a shower. I wait no more than three minutes and, just as I'm about to go back to my room, the door opens. Before me stands a Dominican boy –– big, young, handsome, with that bad boy attitude. I avoid his glance and say «Excuse me,» as I go in to take a shower. Then when I'm done I go back to my room.

The bar was good last night. I made my coins. I call the Malecón for them to deliver a grilled steak with black beans, flan, and a materva with a lot of ice. It's Sunday and I don't want to go outside yet. Maybe later. As I waited for my food, I heard the new arrival leave his room, lock it, and pass by mine with heavy steps. Sure of himself. The food comes. I eat it up. More like I swallow it. I can't lie down –– I don't want to get bloated again. I go out to get a coffee. Coming down the stairs from the second

con el nuevo vecino. Viene subiendo. Se me pone al frente y me dice:

–Oye, quiero hablar contigo.

–Voy de salida. Cuando vuelva –le respondo.

Me voy caminando a la bakery que queda más cerca. Este barrio está lleno de bakeries. Voy pensando en qué onda, qué querrá hablar conmigo. Aunque no me pareció agresivo, me pongo nervioso. Mientras camino pienso en lo atractivo que está. Me tomo un café negro acompañado de un pastel de coco piña. Todo por dos dólares. Sólo aquí en Washington Heights se pueden encontrar cosas baratas. Yo diría que éste es el único lugar de Manhattan en el que los que no tenemos mucho dinero todavía podemos vivir. Camino por ahí. Window shopping. Siempre hago window shopping los domingos. Vuelvo a mi cuarto. Antes voy al baño y cuando salgo me cruzo con el chico de al lado.

Respiro profundo y le pregunto que qué es lo que tiene que hablar conmigo y me dice:

–Oye, no me tengas miedo. Yo trabajo aquí a la vuelta, en el punto de cocaine.

–Todo cool. No problem. Hablamos.

Y me meto a mi cuarto. Me echo en la cama, y pienso en lo buena onda que es mi vecino, y en lo bueno que está. Cuerpazo. Masculine. Ojos como achinados, pero grandes y castaños. Labios gruesos, diría frutosos. Y me entretengo pensando en cómo tendrá

floor, I run across my new neighbor. He's on his way upstairs. He stands in front of me and says, «Hey, I wanna talk to you.»

«I'm on my way out. When I get back,» I answer.

I walk out to the closest bakery. This neighborhood is full of bakeries. I'm wondering what's up with him, what could he want to talk to me about. He didn't seem aggressive, but still I start to get nervous. As I walk I think about how attractive he is. I have a black coffee and a coconut pineapple cake. Both for two dollars. Only here in Washington Heights can you find things so cheap. It's the only place in Manhattan, I'd say, where those of us who don't have a lot of money can still live. I walk around. Window shopping. I always go window shopping on Sundays. I go back to my room. But first I go to the bathroom and when I come out I run into the boy next door.

I take a deep breath and ask him what he wants to talk to me about and he tells me, «Hey, don't be scared. I work around the corner, at the cocaine spot.»

«Todo cool. No problem. We'll talk.»

And I go into my room and close the door. I lie down on the bed, and think what a cool neighbor I have. Lo bueno que está. Body to die for. Masculine. Slanted eyes, but big and brown. Thick lips, juicy even. And I entertain myself thinking about

43

la verga. Me quedo dormido. Los domingos no salgo a trabajar. Duermo hasta el otro día. Me despierto a la mañana, para variar con hambre. Ya no me queda tanto dinero, así que no estoy para pedir delivery. Voy a un restaurant chino. Chicken in garlic sauce plus the soda, por sólo cinco dólares. Antes de volver a mi cuarto paso a comprar algunas frutas, mi infaltable aguacate y dos heros de pan integral. Me echo en la cama a ver televisión. Siento cómo el chico de al lado sale de su cuarto y se va a la calle. Vuelve rápido. Seguro que también fue a comprar comida. Ésta noche tengo que salir a la barra. Me tomo una siesta y despierto como a las seis. Me voy a la cocina a moler el aguacate para comérmelo con el pan integral, acompañado de una taza de té. Vuelvo a mi cuarto y me lo devoro. Voy a la cocina a lavar el plato con restos de aguacate. De vuelta por el pasillo siento un ¡ps, ps! bien despacio. Y veo que la puerta del cuarto del chico de al lado está entreabierta. Asoma su cabeza y me hace gestos para que vaya. Abro la puerta, veo que está completamente desnudo. Me quedo asombrado. Sin pensarlo le pregunto si quiere que le mame la verga. Él me dice que sí. Yo, en la onda de más sabe el diablo por viejo que por diablo, le dejo claro que no le voy a dar nada, que no tengo dinero. Él me dice que no con la cabeza. Me pongo de rodillas. Dejo los platos en el suelo, que hacen ruido desde hace rato por el nerviosismo que tengo. Él

what his cock must be like. I fall asleep. Sundays I don't work. I sleep all day, into the next. I wake up in the morning, hungry. What's new. I don't have that much money left, so I can't order delivery. I go to a Chinese restaurant. Chicken in garlic sauce plus the soda, for just five dollars. Before going back up to my room I go buy some fruit, an avocado since I can never be without one, and two loaves of whole wheat bread. I lie down in bed to watch TV. I can hear the boy next door leave his room and go outside. He comes back quickly. He must have gone out to get food too. Tonight I have to go to the bar. I take a nap and get up at like six. I go to the kitchen to mash the avocado so I can eat it on the wheat bread, with a cup of tea. I go back to my room and devour it. I go to the kitchen to wash the bits of smeared avocado off the plate. Coming back through the hallway, I hear a slow pssst! And I see that the boy next door's door is cracked open. He sticks his head out and motions for me to come in. I open the door and see that he's completely naked. I'm shocked. Without even thinking, I ask him if he wants me to suck his cock. He says yes. And to show that I've been around the block a few times, I make it very clear that I am not going to give him anything for it, because I have no money. He shakes his head no. I get on my knees. I put down the plates that have been

acerca su miembro a mi boca. Yo la abro y comienzo a mamar con la mayor inspiración y concentración que puedo. Siento cómo él hace gemidos de puro placer. Le digo que se tienda en la cama y sigo mamando hasta que explota en mi boca. Boto el semen en el plato que antes tenía aguacate. Sin decir nada salgo de su cuarto. Con cuidado. No me vaya a ver la dueña del departamento. Me siento en mi cama, aún incrédulo de lo que ha pasado. No me cabe en la cabeza que un muchacho que podría ser mi hijo me haya dejado mamarlo sin pedirme nada a cambio. Veo el semen en el plato. Es blanco y espeso. Pienso que así debe ser el semen de los caballos. Me echo hacia atrás. Me masturbo, y me vengo como hace mucho tiempo no me venía. Esa noche me voy a la barra y vuelvo como siempre, algo después de las cuatro de la madrugada. Había sido una noche regular. Me había hecho como unos ochenta dólares. Todo en propinas. No estaba tan mal para ser un día lunes. Ya me había sacado todo el maquillaje y, cuando estaba listo para acostarme, siento que alguien abre la puerta del departamento. Sé que es el chico de al lado. Me acuesto y a los minutos siento golpecitos en la pared que separa nuestros cuartos. Me levanto y voy donde él. La puerta está medio abierta. Entro, él está echado en la cama con las piernas abiertas y el miembro erecto. Sin decir palabras subo a la cama, comienzo a mamar. Explota dentro y, con

clattering in my nervous hands. He puts himself up to my mouth. I open and start to suck with all the concentration and inspiration I can. I can hear him moan with pleasure. I tell him to lie flat and I keep sucking until he explodes in my mouth. I spit the semen onto the plate that had had the avocado on it. I leave his room without a word. Carefully. Can't let the landlady see me. I sit down on my bed, still not believing what just happened. I can't get over the fact that a boy young enough to be my son let me suck him off without asking for anything in return. I see the semen on the plate. It's thick and white. I think, this is what horse semen must look like. I lie back. I masturbate, and I come like I haven't come in a long time. That night I go off to the bar and come back like always, after four in the morning. It'd been an OK night. I'd made something like eighty dollars. All in tips. Not too bad for a Monday. I had already taken off all my make-up and, when I was ready to get into bed I hear someone opening an apartment door. I know it's the boy from next door. I go to bed and a few minutes later I hear a faint tapping from the other side of the wall between our rooms. I get up and go over to him. The door is half open. I go in, and he's lying on the bed, erect, with his legs spread. Without saying a word I get into bed, and start to suck. He explodes and with my mouth still

la boca llena, me regreso a mi cuarto. Sentado en la cama abro la boca, dejo caer el semen en mis manos y me doy un facial.

Y así fueron casi todos los días. Ya sabía que su turno en el punto de coca terminaba a las cinco de la madrugada. Lo sentía llegar y no esperaba ni cinco minutos para sentir los golpecitos en la pared. Automáticamente me iba a su cuarto a mamarle la verga. Una de esas tantas veces cuando estábamos en su cama, me dio por cambiar de posición, poniendo mis pies hacia su cabeza. De pronto siento cómo él me toca la verga y, sin darme cuenta, la tengo dentro de su boca. Así fue de ahí en adelante. Hacíamos sesentinueve. Cada día a las cinco de la madrugada estaba a su espera. Estaba absolutamente enchulado. Y así pasaron los días, aunque debiera decir las noches. A veces era yo quien tocaba la pared. No hablábamos absolutamente nada. Los dos nos veníamos juntos.

Creo que ya había llegado el otoño. Despierto temprano. Alguien mete mucho ruido en el cuarto de al lado. Me levanto y voy al baño, más en la onda de averiguar lo que estaba pasando. Un tipo que nunca había visto estaba vaciando el cuarto del chico de al lado. Él no estaba. Le pregunto a la señora qué es lo que estaba pasando. Ella me cuenta que a mi vecino se lo habían llevado preso. Seguro que lo agarraron en el punto, me digo para mis adentros. Vuelvo a mi cuarto

full I go back to my room. Sitting on my bed I open my mouth, let the semen fall onto my hands, and I give myself a facial.

This is how it went almost every day. I knew that his shift at the cocaine spot ended at five in the morning. I heard him get back and I didn't have to wait five minutes before I heard the quiet tapping on the wall. Automatically I went to his room to suck him off. One of these times that we were in his bed, I shifted position for some reason, putting my feet towards his head. Suddenly I feel him touching my cock and before I realize it, he has it in his mouth. That's how it went from there on out. We sixty-nined. Every day at five in the morning I was waiting. I had it bad for him, real bad. And so the days went by, or rather the nights. Sometimes I was the one who tapped on the wall. We never said one word. We always came together.

I think it was already into the fall. I get up early. Someone is making a lot of noise in the room next door. I get up and go to the bathroom, really just to figure out what was going on. A guy I had never seen was emptying out the room of the boy next door. He wasn't there. I ask the lady what's going on. She tells me that they've arrested my neighbor. They must have nabbed him at the cocaine spot, I tell myself. I come back to my room and flop down

y me echo en la cama para seguir durmiendo. Pensaba en cómo iba a extrañar esos sesentinueve y esa verga que era como una fruta dentro de mi boca.

Ni me acuerdo quién llegó a rentar el cuarto. Quizás habría pasado un año. Entre otoño e invierno, día de semana. Había vuelto de la barra como siempre algo después de las cuatro. Estoy ya en la cama cuando siento suaves golpes en la pared de mi cuarto, que da al pasillo del segundo piso. La puerta de mi cuarto está casi pegada a la puerta del departamento. En vez de no hacer caso a la insistencia de los golpes en la pared y tratar de dormir, me da por levantarme y abrir la puerta. Era él. Me sonríe. Le sonrío. Lo meto a mi cuarto. Nos besamos. Antes nunca nos habíamos besado. Nos desnudamos. Me voy directo a su verga. Él me acaricia la calva. Hacemos el sesenta y nueve. Nos venimos juntos. Nos relajamos. Le pregunto por qué lo habían agarrado. Me contó que había incumplido su parole. Me contó que era la tercera vez que caía preso. Se viste y se va. Me dormí con una sonrisa en los labios.

Pasó casi un mes sin que lo viera, hasta que una noche como de costumbre llegó a tocarme la pared. De un salto me levanto de la cama. Le abro y de un agarrón lo meto dentro de mi cuarto. Nos besamos. Y no sé cómo pasó: antes de irme directo a su verga, me dio por besarle el cuello y de ahí su

to go back to sleep. I thought about how I would miss those sixty-nines and that cock that was like fruit in my mouth.

I don't even remember who ended up renting the room. Maybe a year went by. Between fall and winter: a weekday. I had come back from the bar a little after four, as always. I'm already in bed when I hear soft knocks on one of the walls, the one that separates me from the second floor hallway. The door to my room is right up against the front door of the whole apartment. Instead of ignoring the insistent knocks on the wall and just trying to sleep, I decide to get up and open the door. It was him. He smiles at me. I smile at him. I bring him into my room. We kiss. Before, we had never kissed. We get naked. I go right for his cock. He caresses my bald spot. We sixty-nine. We come together. We relax. I ask him why they had nabbed him. He told me he'd violated his parole. He told me it was the third time he got put away. He gets dressed and leaves. I fell asleep with a smile on my lips.

Almost a month went by with no sight of him until one night, as usual, he came and knocked on my wall. I jump out of bed. I open the door to grab him and pull him into my room. We kiss. I don't know how it happened: before going right for his cock, for some reason I kissed his neck and went on kissing

51

espalda. Terminé penetrándolo. Nos vinimos como siempre con el sesentinueve. Se viste y se va sin decir palabra. Como siempre. Me siento como en una especie de limbo. La sensación de haber penetrado a ese hermoso caballo me había dejado sin aliento. Antes de dormirme me acordé de algo que había visto en él. Algo que me incomodaba. Se veía algo demacrado y parece que había perdido bastante peso. Me dormí. Esa noche me había hecho buen dinero, así que decidí no salir ese día. Me daría un break en medio de la semana. Cool. Sabía que esa noche no podría dormir. Como a eso de las diez de la noche me fui al punto a comprar un veinte de coca. Llego, y el que abre la puerta del building donde se vende el material es el chico de al lado. Se puso muy nervioso. Yo diría que se sonrojó. Ya en mi cuarto, después de dos jales, me dio por pensar que en realidad se veía demacrado y que sí había perdido bastante peso.

Es ya de madrugada y me voy a comprar dos cigarros sueltos al grocery. El cigarro me ayuda a bajar la nota. Caminando bien abrigado, pues ya hacía mucho frío, veo que él está en una esquina cantando a todo pulmón. Tiene los audífonos puestos. Quizás por eso no escucha lo fuerte que está cantando. Había algo extraño en su comportamiento. Cuando volví de comprar los looses ya no estaba. Fumando me puse

his back. I ended up penetrating him. We came like we always did, together. He gets dressed and leaves without saying a word. Like always. I feel like I'm in some kind of limbo. The feeling of penetrating this beautiful horse of a man had left me breathless. Before I fell asleep I remembered something I had seen in him. Something that made me uncomfortable. He looked kind of emaciated, as if he had lost a lot of weight. I fell asleep. That night I'd made some good money, so I decided not to go out that day. I would give myself a little break in the middle of the week. Cool. I knew that I wouldn't be able to sleep that night. Around ten at night I went to the spot to buy a twenty bag of blow. I get there, and the guy who opens the front door of the building where they sell the goods is the boy from next door. He got real nervous. I'd even say he blushed. Back in my room, after two lines, I got to thinking that he really did look emaciated and that he'd lost a lot of weight.

It's almost dawn already and I'm headed to the grocery to buy two loosies. Cigarettes help me come down from coke. Walking in my warm coat, because it was getting really cold, I see that he's out on the corner singing at the top of his lungs. He has his earphones in. So maybe he can't tell how loud he's singing. There was something strange in the way he was acting. When I came back from buying the loosies he wasn't

a pensar que si venía esta noche o cualquier otra lo iba a regañar. Que se le notaba que estaba haciendo alguna droga. Que me tenía que escuchar. Que yo era mayor que él. Pero volvió a desaparecer. Quizás se lo habían llevado nuevamente preso. Por lo menos se va a desintoxicar, pensé. Un día en la cocina, como siempre moliendo aguacate, la dueña de casa me comenta que hace semanas que no había visto al chico que vivía antes al lado de mi cuarto. Yo, como haciéndome el tonto, le pregunto de quién, de entre toda la gente que ella ha rentado ese cuarto, me está hablando. Ella se ríe como diciéndome no te hagas. Yo la dejo hablar.

–Lo veía casi todos los días cuando iba a comprar algo a la tienda. Pero hace un tiempo que no aparece. Seguro que se lo llevaron preso de nuevo. Pobre muchacho. Yo lo conozco desde que era un chamaquito.

Yo la miro asombrado.

–Creía que usted lo había conocido cuando había venido a vivir acá.

–No, para nada. Él vivía en el building de acá a la vuelta con su abuela. Su mamá desapareció. Nunca más se supo de ella. Tampoco tiene papá. La abuela se enfermó y se la llevaron a un home. Así que él se quedó solo. Siempre renta un cuarto aquí en el barrio. Siempre vuelve para acá después que sale de la cárcel, el pobre.

there anymore. While I smoked I got to thinking that if he came by tonight or any other night I would give him a good talking-to. I would tell him that everyone can tell he's on some kind of drugs. That he had to listen to me –– I was older than him. But he disappeared again. Maybe they had arrested him again. At least he'll detox that way, I thought. One day in the kitchen, mashing up avocado like usual, the landlady told me how it had been weeks since she'd seen the boy who used to live in the room next to mine. Playing stupid, I asked her which boy she was talking about, out of all the people who had rented that room. She laughs as if to say, stop the act. I let her speak.

«I would see him almost every day when I went out to buy something at the store. But he hasn't shown up in a good while. They must have locked him up again. Pobre muchacho. I've known him since he was just a little chamaquito.»

I look at her, shocked. «I thought you had just met him when he came to live here.»

«No, para nada. He used to live around the corner with his grandmother. His mom disappeared. No one heard from her ever again. No dad, either. His grandmother got sick and they took her away to a home. So he was left on his own. He always rents a room here in the neighborhood. He always comes back around here when he gets out of jail, el pobre.»

Volví a mi cuarto. Por primera vez el aguacate no me supo a nada. Me tomé el té y me eché en la cama. Pensaba en el chico de al lado. En las ganas de tenerlo al lado mío. En por qué no le había dado mi número telefónico. Le hubiera dicho que se lo memorizara. Así me habría podido llamar de la cárcel o del detox. Le habría podido mandar aunque fueran unos veinte dólares. Me dormí excitado y algo cansado. Me dormí pensando en él.

Pasó el invierno y volvió rápido, como siempre en Nueva York. Ya hace casi un año que no iba a las barras. Me había puesto en la onda cibernética. Ponía avisos en la internet. Como mi cuarto quedaba al lado de la puerta del departamento, podía meter clientes sin que nadie se diera cuenta. En especial de noche, cuando todos dormían. Igual la señora después de un tiempo se dio cuenta. Y buena onda, pues me dijo:

—Mientras tú me pagues el cuarto a mí no me importa.

Así que siempre le estoy dando algunos chelitos para que se compre sus cigarros sueltos. Era un sábado, algo después de la medianoche. Era principio de invierno. Salgo a comprarme una bolsa de coca. Abro la puerta y me lo encuentro a él. A punto de tocar mi pared. Inmediatamente le digo que vuelva más tarde. Que aún la señora no se dormía. Nos damos una sonrisa cómplice. Estaba realmente guapo. Se veía más

I went back to my room. For the first time, the avocado had no flavor. I drank my tea and lay down in bed. I was thinking about the boy from next door, about how I wanted him beside me. Why hadn't I given him my phone number. I should have told him to memorize it. That way he could have called me from jail or from detox. I could have sent him even just like twenty dollars. I fell asleep horny and kind of tired. I fell asleep thinking about him.

Winter ended and returned quickly, as it always does in New York. I hadn't been out to the bars in almost a year. I had gotten into the whole online thing. I posted ads on the internet. Since my room was next to the main door, I could let clients in without anyone knowing. Especially at night when everyone was asleep. Even then, after a while the lady realized what was going on. But she's cool so she told me, «As long as you pay your rent, it doesn't matter to me.»

So I'm always giving her some extra chelitos so she can buy herself loosies. It was a Saturday, a little after midnight. It was the start of winter. I go out to buy a bag of blow. I open the door and there he is. About to knock on my door. Immediately I tell him to come back later –– the lady isn't asleep yet. We exchange a knowing smile. He was really looking nice. Like more of a man than a boy. I think I was

hombre. Yo también creo que me veía mejor. Había bajado de peso, pues ya no iba a las barras, así que ya no tomaba alcohol ni cuando me echaba coca, como esa noche. Pura agua. Me pongo a contestar el teléfono. Me hago un cliente. No me vengo. Quiero guardarme para el chico de al lado.

Él llegó como siempre después de las cuatro. Sentí los golpecitos en la pared. Abrí la puerta y apenas estuvo en mi cuarto nos devoramos a besos. Hicimos el sesentinueve y lo penetré. Antes de que se fuera le pregunté si quería mi número telefónico. Lo marcó en su celular. Como siempre se fue sin decir palabra.

Ese invierno parecía que venía a quedarse por un buen tiempo. Y así fue. Llegó la navidad y, por suerte, yo con algo de dinero. No hay nada peor que una navidad sin dinero. Cuando compraba coca ya no iba al punto de la vuelta. Había encontrado que en la otra esquina la vendían más barata. Así que rara vez veía al chico de al lado. Algunas veces sólo a lo lejos. Y tampoco había aparecido a tocarme la pared. Era noche de año nuevo y yo venía llegando de donde Diana, una amiga hondureña con la que nos habíamos tomado una botella entera de Bacardí. Por supuesto, con Coca Cola. No estaba borracho, pues había consumido cocaine. Estaba tendido en la cama cuando suena mi celular. Lo contesto de inmediato, pensando que puede ser algún cliente.

looking better too. I had lost weight since I didn't go to the bars anymore, so I wasn't drinking alcohol –– not even when I did blow, like that night. Just water. I start answering my messages. I get a client. I don't come with him. I want to save myself for the boy from next door.

He showed up like always, after four. I felt the soft tapping on the wall. I opened the door and as soon as he stepped inside we devoured each other in kisses. We sixty-nined and I penetrated him. Before he could leave I asked him if he wanted my phone number. He saved it in his phone. Like always he left without another word.

That winter it seemed like he had come to stay for a good long while. And that's how it went. Christmas came and, luckily, I had some money. There's nothing worse than a Christmas with no money. When I bought coke I didn't go to the spot around the corner anymore. I'd found out they sold it cheaper on the other corner. So I hardly ever saw the boy from next door. A few times from a distance. And he hadn't come by to knock on the wall, either. It was New Year's Eve and I was on my way home from my Honduran friend Diana's, where we had downed a whole bottle of Bacardi. With Coca-Cola, of course. I wasn't drunk, because I'd had some cocaine. I was stretched out in bed when my cell rings. I answer it right away, thinking it could be a client.

Genial, pensé. Borrachitos, de seguro. Y así es más fácil que suelten la billetera. Pero no. Al momento que contesto alguien me dice que quiere pasar la noche conmigo. Pregunto quién es. Me responde que el que antes vivía al lado. Que yo le había dado mi número telefónico. Sonrío y le digo que claro. Me cuenta que se va a demorar algo en llegar. Que está esperando a un amigo que le va a dar yerba. Me levanto y empiezo a arreglar la cama. Sé que vamos a estar más tiempo juntos. Más que las otras veces. Pasa menos de una hora. Sin llamarme, vuelve a tocarme la pared. Le abro y, sin decirnos feliz año nuevo, deposita en el suelo un six pack de cervezas. Saca una para él y otra para mí. Las destapa con los dientes. Toma un sorbo y comienza a enrolar un blont. Lo prende y comenzamos a fumar. Mientras se desnuda saca de uno de los bolsillos del pantalón una bolsa de coca. La deja sobre la cama y, mientras sigue bebiendo su cerveza, me mira sonriendo. Sabe que estoy feliz con el regalo. La muelo y me doy una raya. Le ofrezco. Él no acepta. Entiendo que debe estar en parole y que de seguro le hacen exámenes de orina. Bebo de mi cerveza mientras él se echa de espaldas en mi cama con el miembro bien parado. Yo, que con la coca y la yerba me vuelvo bien kinky, le pongo coca en la cabeza del pene. Comienzo a mamar mientras él se queja de placer. Tomo cerveza, que aún está fría y sigo mamando, causándole más placer a causa del cambio

Great, I thought. They're probably drunk. At least that way they're not so tight with their wallets. But no. As soon as I answer someone is telling me he wants to spend the night with me. I ask who it is. He tells me that it's him, the one who used to live next door. I had given him my number, in case I didn't remember. I smile and say oh yeah of course. He tells me it will take him a while to get here. He's waiting for a friend who's going to give him some weed. I get up and start making the bed. I know we're going to be together longer. Longer than the other times. Less than an hour goes by. Without calling first, he knocks on the wall. I open up and without saying Happy New Year he puts down a sixpack of beers. He takes one out for himself and one for me. He takes the caps off with his teeth. He takes a swig and starts rolling a blunt. He lights it and we start to smoke. As he's getting undressed he takes a bag of blow out of one of his pockets. He leaves it on the bed and as he keeps drinking his beer, he looks at me with a smile on his face. He knows I'm happy with the gift. I crush it up and do a line. I offer some to him. He doesn't take it. I figure he must be on parole and they must give him urine tests. I drink my beer as he lays back on my bed, already fully erect. Now when I have blow and weed I get real kinky, so I put some coke on the head of his penis. I start to suck as he moans with pleasure. I have some

de temperatura que tengo en la boca. De pronto se levanta y se pone al borde de la cama, dándome a entender que me ponga en cuatro. Que me va a penetrar. Excitado y pensando en lo grande que tiene la verga, me doy otro pase. Me pongo en posición y comienza a darme. Al principio suave y después cada vez más fuerte. Siento cómo se viene dentro de mí. Sus gemidos hacen que también me venga. Nos desplomamos. Uno al lado del otro. Después de unos minutos él comienza a fumar de nuevo, mientras yo me doy el pase de cocaine que queda. Bebemos las dos últimas cervezas. Me dice que se tiene que ir. Le pregunto dónde está viviendo. Él contesta everywhere. Se va. Me quedo en una especie de limbo. A pesar de la yerba, la coca y las cervezas, sé que la sensación de high que tengo es por la penetrada que me han dado. Una especie de placer y dolor. Me duermo. Despierto con frío. El cuarto no tiene calefacción y, como yo vengo de clima frío, no me importa. Pero ese invierno estaba fuerte. Pienso en que tengo que comprar un calefactor. Ahorrando un par de días lo consigo. Aun me siento adolorido en la parte de atrás. Me ducho con agua bien caliente. Me doy masajes en el ano. Parece que lo tengo irritado. Pienso en el placer que me dio ser penetrado por esa verga que había mamado tantas veces.

Días después tocan a la puerta de mi cuarto. Era la señora para comentarme lo molesta que estaba,

beer, still cold, and keep sucking, giving him even more pleasure because of the change in temperature I have in my mouth. All of a sudden he gets up and positions himself on the edge of the bed, signaling me to get on all fours. So he could penetrate me. All worked up and thinking about how big his cock is, I do another bump. I assume the position and he starts giving it to me. Gentle at first and then harder and harder. I feel him coming inside me. His moans make me come too. We collapse onto the bed. Side by side. After a few minutes he starts to smoke again, while I do the last remaining bump. We drink down the last two beers. He tells me he has to go. I ask him where he's living. Everywhere, he says. He leaves. I'm left in a kind of limbo. In spite of the weed, the coke, and the beers, I know the high feeling I have is because of how it felt being penetrated by him. A kind of pleasure and pain. I fall asleep. I wake up cold. The room has no heat and since I come from a cold climate I don't mind. But that winter was harsh. I need to buy a heater, I think. If I save up for a few days I can get one. My backside still hurts. I take a nice hot shower. I massage my anus. It feels irritated. I think about how pleasurable it was to be penetrated by that cock I had sucked so many times.

Days later I hear knocking on the door to my room. It was the lady coming to tell me how upset she was that

pues el señor que ahora vivía en el cuarto de al lado se había ido por la noche, debiéndole dos semanas de renta. Le comento que ese tipo nunca me había dado confianza. Me dice que va a llamar a la agencia para ponerlo de nuevo en renta. Se va. Me acuerdo del chico de al lado. Le contaría que el cuarto se había desocupado. Que de seguro la señora se lo rentaba. Que lo conocía desde niño y que no le importaba que pasara preso. Su hijo, de hecho, también estaba preso. Mientras buscaba su número pensaba en lo bueno que sería tenerlo nuevamente de vecino. Que nos podríamos conocer más. Que no conocía ni su nombre. Que seguiríamos siendo amigos con beneficios. Encuentro su número. Lo marco. Aparece una grabación diciendo que ese número está fuera de servicio. Marco de nuevo. Quizás marqué mal algún dígito. Otra vez sale la grabadora. Me echo en la cama. Seguro que cayó preso de nuevo.

Han pasado varios meses. Ya viene el verano. Se nota que va a ser bien húmedo. Me digo que, la vez que vuelva a verlo, lo voy a obligar a aprenderse de memoria mi número telefónico. Que cuando lo agarren otra vez me puede llamar y yo le podría mandar aunque sea veinte dólares.

the man who was living in the room next door now had up and left in the middle of the night, still owing her two weeks' rent. I tell her that guy never seemed like you could trust him. She says she's going to call the agency to put it up for rent again. She leaves. I remember the boy from next door. I could tell him that the room was unoccupied, that the lady would rent it to him for sure. Because she had known him since he was little and she didn't care that he'd been in jail. Her own son was in jail too, actually. As I looked for his number I thought about how good it would be to have him as my neighbor again. About how we could get to know each other better. About how I didn't even know his name. About how we could go on being amigos con beneficios. I find his number. I dial. I get a recording saying that number is out of service. I dial again. Maybe I had mistyped one of the digits. Again the recording. I lie down on the bed. They had locked him up again for sure.

Several months have gone by. Summer is almost here. You can tell it's going to be a really humid one. I tell myself that the next time I see him, I am going to make him learn my phone number by heart. I'll tell him that the next time they catch him he can call me and I could send him even just like twenty dollars.

Un slave

*Él era lo que podríamos llamar un slave. Me cuenta
que es manager de una gran tienda de ropa, que tiene
a más de cien personas a su cargo. Algo así como el big
boss. Se pasa dando órdenes todo el día, de nueve a cinco, que hagan esto, que hagan lo otro. Casi treinta años
en el mismo oficio, y los años que aún le queden por venir. Porque si algo hay cierto acerca de este país es que
la gente trabaja hasta que se muere. No sé si porque lo
necesiten económicamente o porque se tienen que sentir útiles en este engranaje maquinal, en el que cuando
te detienes no tienes derecho a la contemplación o al
goce, sin más opción que la de desaparecer.*

*Era medianoche de un día viernes. Él llegó al bar
donde voy casi todas las noches a buscar mi dinero. Llegó con la idea de ser un slave, de ser él quien recibiera las
órdenes. Necesitaba buscar a un master, aunque en esta
ocasión se había decidido por una mistress, y qué mejor
que un travesti, un hombre vestido de mujer. Una mujer
que al ser hombre inspirase un aire de respeto, que crea-
ra una atmósfera en la que él-ella fuera quien diera las*

A Slave

He was what you could call a slave. He tells me how he's the manager of a big clothing store, how he has more than a hundred people working under him. He spends the whole day giving orders, nine to five, you do this, you do that. Almost thirty years in the same job, plus however many years he has left there. Because if there's one thing that's true about this country, it's that people work until they die. I don't know if they need it for economic reasons or if they need to feel like a useful cog in this big machine in which you can't even stop and think or enjoy anything and the only way to stop is to disappear.

It was midnight on a Friday. He came to the bar I go to almost every night to try and make my money. He came thinking he wanted to be a slave, to be the one receiving the orders. He needed to find a master, although this time he had settled on a mistress, and what better than a travesti, a man dressed as a woman. A woman who, being a man, commanded respect, created an atmosphere in which he/she was the

órdenes. *Era viernes por la noche, y a mí se me había ocurrido ponerme el vestido de leather negro. Botas de igual material y color, con un tacón puntiagudo y metálico. Este tipo de taco era muy bueno, no sólo en lo estético sino para defenderse de más de algún ataque callejero. Me había maquillado en la onda severa, entre la cosa directora de reclusorio y gothic girl. Esa noche me hice llamar Helga. La peluca era rubia nórdica y me llegaba un poco más debajo de los hombros. Hablaba con un acento sumado al acento que ya tengo. Un inglés bien sui generis, así es el inglés de Nueva York. Un inglés de viernes por la noche en un pick up bar. Me senté en la barra del primer piso, la que queda junto a la entrada. Me instalé cerca del televisor, sabiendo que la luz de la pantalla me daría una iluminación misteriosa, pronunciando el maquillaje púrpura de mis ojos y labios. Ahí me quedé como una estatua. Sin sonreír. Las otras travestis que me veían comentaban entre sí. Seguro que los chismes de siempre. Que me estaba volviendo loca, que tanta droga, que tanto alcohol. Fuck all of them! Y ahí estaba yo cuando lo vi acercarse lentamente, con timidez, como corresponde a un slave. Me ofreció un trago. Seriamente contesté:*

–I don't drink.

En un volumen bien despacio me pregunta si puede sentarse cerca de mí. Yo me hago la que no le entiendo,

one giving the orders. It was Friday night, and I had had the idea to wear my black leather dress. Boots of the same material and color, with a pointed metallic heel. This type of heel was very good, not just for aesthetic reasons but also to defend myself in case I was attacked in the street. I had given myself a severe look with my make-up, somewhere between prison warden and goth girl. That night my name was Helga. My wig was Nordic blonde, and it reached down to below my shoulders. I spoke with fake accent on top of the accent I already have. A very idiosyncratic English, which is the way English is in New York anyway. English for a Friday night in a pick-up bar. I sat down at the first-floor bar, the one next to the front door. I set up next to the TV, knowing that the screen would provide a very mysterious lighting scheme, highlighting the purple painted on my eyes and lips. There I sat like a statue. Not smiling. The other travestis who saw me there were talking among themselves. Probably the same gossip as usual. About how I was going crazy, so many drugs, so much alcohol. ¡Jódanse todas! And there I was when I saw him slowly approaching me, timidly, as befits a slave. He offered me a drink. I answered him in a serious tone of voice, «I don't drink.»

Very softly he asks me if he can sit near me. I act like I can't hear him, he has to speak up. Nervously,

que tiene que hablar más fuerte. Nerviosamente, y con voz temblorosa, vuelve a repetir la pregunta. Le digo que sí, pero que no muy cerca, que mantenga cierta distancia. Nuevamente me ofrece un trago. Yo, que muero de ganas por un scotch on the rocks, recuerdo que debo mantenerme en el personaje y le repito que no bebo alcohol. Sabía que él era un slave. Uno de tantos que hay por ahí, y que necesitan los servicios de una mistress.

Esa noche yo era mistress Helga vestida de leather negro y de pelo rubio nórdico. Sin mirarme a los ojos, casi susurrando, me cuenta su historia. Una historia que se repite. Ese hombre necesitaba balancearse, y me correspondía a mí equilibrar sus emociones. Él hablaba y hablaba. Yo lo dejo desahogarse. Y es que en realidad no lo escucho, pues ya sé lo que cuenta. No se diferencia de otras historias. Slave's stories. De pronto lo interrumpo y le digo que no tengo mucho tiempo, que mi tiempo es muy valioso. Abro mi cartera y la pongo cerca de él. Saca un billete de cincuenta dólares y lo pone dentro de esa imitación de Prada adquirida en Chinatown.

–Don't move from here –le digo.

Me pongo de pie y me voy por ahí a conversar con algunas colegas. Lo dejo solo. Sé que él me va esperar. Además le ordeno no hablar con nadie más, no sin antes darle una cachetada entre suave y agresiva en la mejilla. Vuelvo a los quince minutos. Y, como ya sabía,

his voice trembling, he asks me again. I tell him he can, but not too close, he has to maintain a certain distance. Again he offers me a drink. I'm dying for a scotch on the rocks but I remember I have to keep the character up so I repeat that I don't drink alcohol. I knew he was a slave. One of so many others around that place, in need of the services of a mistress.

That night I was Mistress Helga, dressed in black leather and Nordic blonde wig. Without looking me in the eyes, almost in a whisper, he tells me his story. One I've heard before. That man needed to balance himself out, and I was going to be the one to set his emotional scale even again. He talked and talked. So I let him get everything off his chest. Actually I'm not even listening, because I already know what he's saying. Nothing different from other stories. Slaves' stories. All of a sudden I interrupt him and tell him I don't have much time, and my time is very valuable. I open my purse and put it next to him. He takes out a fifty-dollar bill and puts it inside that Prada knock-off I got in Chinatown.

«Don't move from here,» I tell him.

I get up and go over to talk with some other girls. I leave him alone. I know he will wait for me. I also order him not to talk to anyone else, giving him a slap on the cheek that is somewhere between soft and aggressive. I come back fifteen minutes later. And, just

71

ahí está él. En el mismo lugar y con la misma actitud, encorvado. Me acerco y le doy otra cachetada, algo más fuerte que la anterior.

–I'm your mistress and you're my slave. We'll go to your home right now! –le ordeno.

–Yes, mistress –contesta.

Salimos del bar y tomamos un taxi al East Side.

–Seventy Third and Second Avenue –le dice al taxista.

El área del dinero, pienso para mis adentros. Le pregunto si no tiene que pasar a un cajero automático. Él dice que no. Que no me preocupe. Llegamos a su departamento ubicado en el décimo piso. Es un lugar amplio, decorado sin gusto personal. Lo que yo llamaría decoración de catálogo. Todo es de aspecto utilitario. No aguanto más y le pregunto si tiene scotch.

–Yes, mistress.

Y corre a la cocina, desde donde vuelve con un vaso lleno de hielo. Va a un mueble y saca una botella de Johnnie Walker. Y sí, era blue label. Se la arrebato. Me sirvo una, me sirvo dos veces. Estoy lista para seguir con esta representación. Me siento en el sillón que se ve más cómodo, y alzo mis piernas calzadas con las botas de leather. Él se agacha como un perro y las comienza a lamer, como si las lustrara con su lengua. Le digo que lama los tacones metálicos. Y esa lengua se hace ofídica. Saco de mi bolso el único cigarrillo que me

as I thought, there he is. In the same place with the same posture, hunched over. I come close and give him another slap, a little harder than the last.

«I'm your mistress and you're my slave. We'll go to your home right now!» I order him.

«Yes, mistress,» he answers.

We leave the bar and take a taxi to the East Side.

«Seventy-third and Second Avenue,» he tells the cabbie.

A neighborhood with money, I think to myself. I ask him if he needs to go by an ATM. He says no, not to worry. We get to his apartment, located on the tenth floor. It's a spacious place, decorated without a personal sense of style. What I could call catalog décor. Everything looks utilitarian. I can't hold out any longer and ask him if he has scotch.

«Yes, mistress.»

He runs to the kitchen and comes back with a glass full of ice. He reaches into a cupboard and takes out a bottle of Johnnie Walker. Ah yes, Blue Label. I snatch it away from him. I pour myself one, I pour myself another. Now I'm ready to keep up this act. I sit in the most comfortable-looking armchair and lift my legs clad in the leather boots. He gets down like a dog and starts licking them, as if he were shining them with his tongue. I tell him to lick the metal heels. And that tongue turns into a serpent's tongue. I

queda. Él corre a buscar un encendedor. Lo enciende y alzo más mis piernas, dándole a entender que necesito su espalda para reposarlas. Se pone en cuatro, como una mesa, y yo las deposito. Mientras fumo le ordeno ladrar. Él ladra. Le ordeno aullar. El aúlla. Antes de terminar de fumar el cigarrillo se lo doy para que lo apague. A pesar de que he dejado las cenizas en su nuca, no puedo ser tan cruel y causarle una quemadura. Cuando vuelve de apagar el cigarrillo le pongo de frente mi cartera abierta. Saca quinientos dólares y los deposita adentro. Me pongo de pie y le ordeno que se baje los pantalones.

–I know you have been a bad boy.

Y comienzo a darle palmadas, cada vez más fuerte hasta que las palmas de las manos se me ponen rojas. Él sabe que me merezco al menos unos doscientos dólares más. Los deposita en mi cartera. Le digo que se tire al piso, boca abajo. Comienzo a pisarlo. Mas bien a pisotearlo, como si fuera uno de esos tapetes que hay en las entradas de las casas, donde te limpias los pies antes de entrar con las palabras «welcome» o «home sweet home». Le digo que se dé vuelta y que abra la boca. Lo orino. Lo obligo a que se la trague. Luego lo escupo. Me alejo un poco de él y le digo que me tengo que ir. Que él es un perro asqueroso y que no merece mi compañía. Antes de irme me pone otros trescientos dólares en la cartera. Me voy sin despedirme. Tomo un taxi.

take my last cigarette out of my bag. He runs to get a lighter. He lights it and I lift my legs higher, signaling him that I need his back to rest them on. He gets on all fours, like a coffee table, and I put them down on him. While I smoke I order him to bark. He barks. I order him to howl. He howls. Before finishing my cigarette I give it to him to put out. Even though I've ashed on the back of his neck, I can't be so cruel as to give him a burn. When he comes back from putting out the cigarette I put my purse out in front of him. He takes out five hundred dollars and deposits them inside. I stand up and order him to drop his pants.

«I know you have been a bad boy.»

And I start to slap him, harder and harder, until my palms turn red. He knows I deserve at least two hundred dollars more. He deposits them in my purse. I tell him to lie down on the floor, face down. I start stepping on him. Or more like stomping on him, as if he were one of those doormats at the front door of a house, where you wipe your feet before going in, the ones with the words «Welcome» or «Home Sweet Home.» I tell him to turn over and open his mouth. I urinate on him. I make him swallow it. Then I spit on him. I step away from him and tell him that I have to go, that he is a disgusting dog who does not deserve my company. Before I leave he puts three hundred dollars more in my purse. I leave without saying good-bye. I take a taxi.

Estoy cansada. Muy cansada. Estoy segura de que él ya está relajado. Alguien le ordenó. Le ordenó a llegar a lo más bajo. Sin importarme lo que diga el taxista, me quito la peluca. Estoy muy agotada. Cuento lo que tengo en la cartera: mil cincuenta dólares. La Prada fake de Chinatown se ha transformado en una Prada original de la Quinta Avenida. Le digo al taxista que me lleve a la calle 146 y Broadway. Al Alto Manhattan, el punto de crack. Necesito fumar por lo menos unos cien dólares, relajarme. Ha sido una noche muy tensa. Una vez más necesito ponerme high y balancear mis emociones.

I am just so, so tired. I am sure that he's relaxed already. Someone ordered him around. Someone ordered him to hit his lowest point. I take my wig off, don't care what the cabbie might say. I am so exhausted. I count what I have in my purse: one thousand fifty dollars. The Prada knock-off from Chinatown has transformed into a Prada original from Fifth Avenue. I tell the cabbie to take me to 146th Street and Broadway. To Upper Manhattan, the crack spot. I need to smoke off at least a hundred dollars or so, to relax. It's been such a tense night. I need to get high and balance my emotions out. One more time.

La misma nota, forever

Voy caminando por el East Village. Es domingo. Hace tiempo que le había prometido a Silvia ayudarla a limpiar su studio. No la veo desde hace mucho, cinco o seis años. Es que un día alguien me llamó por teléfono:

–¿Qué hace?

Así tal cual, como si nos hubiéramos visto ayer.

–¿Qué hace?

Yo sonrío de felicidad al escucharla. Sé de inmediato que es ella.

–Aquí pues, niña. ¿Y tú?

Años atrás vivimos en el mismo neighborhood, el Hell's Kitchen. Años atrás, en el siglo pasado, a fines de los noventa. Nos presentó la Fernando, una colombiana algo mala de los nervios. Eran las seis de la madrugada, calle 43 y Octava Avenida. Mi nueva amiga me invitaba un café.

–Me llamo Silvia Gold.

Después supe que también le decían Silvia Hammer, por la forma de la cabeza.

Never, Ever Ever, Coming Down

I'm walking around the East Village. It's Sunday. It's been a while since I promised Silvia I would help her clean her studio apartment. I haven't seen her in a long time, five or six years. But then one day I got a phone call:

«What up?»

Just like that, as if we had just seen each other yesterday.

«What up?»

I smile, so happy to hear her voice. I know immediately that it's her. «Not much, niña. You?»

Some years back, we lived in the same neighborhood, Hell's Kitchen. Years back, last century already, at the end of the nineties. We were introduced by la Fernando, a Colombian who was a little mala de los nervios. It was six in the morning, 43rd Street and Eighth Avenue. My new friend took me out for a coffee.

«My name is Silvia Gold.»

Later I found out that she also went by Silvia Hammer, on account of the shape of her head.

Nos fuimos caminando al oeste. Hacia el río. Nos detuvimos afuera de un diner. Estaba a punto de amanecer. Me sentía como dentro de un cuadro, uno de Hopper.

–Mira, al lado del diner está el Edelweiss. En esa barra las locas se hacen dinerales.

Y yo pensaba en Sharon Stone lanzando los billetes al cielo en la película Casino.

Me sonrío mientras voy caminando donde Silvia, feliz de verla después de tanto tiempo. Es primavera y es domingo. Igual hace frío. Son como las siete de la tarde. Reviso a cada rato la dirección que tengo anotada en el celular. Últimamente anoto todo lo que pienso que se me puede olvidar, como que me está fallando la memoria. Chequeo la identificación que llevo. No es mía, pero igual me ha servido en más de una oportunidad. Voy repasando la información del ID, en caso de que el guardia tenga dudas. Y es que Silvia vive en una especie de home, eso creo yo.

Antes de entrar al building la llamo.

–Ya estoy entrando.

Ningún problema con el moreno del front desk. Silvia baja a buscarme. Le doy un abrazo bien fuerte. Estoy feliz de volver a verla después de tantos años. Tomamos el elevador hacia el tercer piso. Entramos a su casa. Es un cuarto con una pequeña cocina y un baño independiente: un studio.

We set off towards the west. Towards the river. We stopped outside a diner. Dawn was about to break. I felt like I was in a painting, a Hopper painting.

«Look, that's the Edelweiss next to the diner. The locas make an absolute fortune in that bar.»

And I thought about Sharon Stone throwing dollar bills into the air in the movie Casino.

I'm smiling as I walk toward Silvia's, happy to see her after so long. It's spring, and it's Sunday. Still, it's cold out. It's something like seven in the evening. Every so often I check the address I have saved in my cellphone. Lately I save onto my phone every thought that I might forget, as if my memory is starting to fail me. I check the ID I have on me. It's not mine, but it's come in handy more than once. I keep going over the information on the ID, in case the building guard has any doubts. Because Silvia lives in some kind of a home. I think.

Before going into the building I call her.

«I'm on my way in.»

No problem with the black guy at the front desk. Silvia comes down for me. I give her a big hug. I'm happy to see her after so many years. We take the elevator to the third floor. We go into her place. It's a room with a little kitchen and a separate bath: a studio.

–*Aquí estás divina, pues niña* –le comento mientras ella se echa en la cama.

–*Ay, pero yo no me siento bien* –alega.

Yo la miro.

–*Ay, loca. Please.*

Me acuerdo de los años nuevos que pasábamos en la casa de su hermana en New Jersey. Cómo nos producíamos con el look. Ella en la onda Joan Collins o Shirley Bassey, yo en la onda white woman from Fairfield, Connecticut.

–*Ya, deja de quejarte y déjame empezar a limpiar.*

Empiezo por el baño. Mientras le echo Ajax a la tina le comento cómo me ha ido la vida. Y nada ha cambiado. Desde su cama me dice en voz alta:

–*Es que a ninguna loca con tetas le van a dar trabajo en alguna parte. Por eso no te queda otra cosa que dedicarte al show business.*

Nos largamos a reír.

Bien fuerte con una escobilla dejo la tina brillante.

–*¡Me boté!* –le digo a Silvia, pasando Windex por el espejo y lavamanos.

Más Ajax para el retrete. Y bastante cloro.

–*¡Me estoy botando, loquita!* –digo, caminando hacia la cocina para que los desinfectantes hagan su efecto.

No mucho que hacer. Uno que otro plato sucio.

«This is a fabulous place, niña,» I tell her as she lays down on the bed.

«Ay, but I don't feel so good,» she claims.

I look at her.

«Oh loca. Pleez.»

I remember the many New Years we spent at her sister's house in New Jersey. How we would put our looks together. She'd be serving up Joan Collins or Shirley Bassey, and I'd be giving you white woman from Fairfield, Connecticut.

«Whatever. Stop complaining and let me get cleaning.»

I start with the bathroom. As I'm shaking Ajax into the tub I tell her how it's been going. And nothing has changed. From her bed she tells me loudly:

«It's just that a loca with tits is never going to get a job anywhere. That's why you have no choice but to go into show business.»

We laughed and laughed.

I scrub the tub real good, leaving it nice and shiny.

«I really went all out on that one,» I tell Silvia as I wipe down the mirror and the sink with Windex.

More Ajax for the toilet. And lots of bleach.

«I'm really going all out here, loquita!» I say, walking over to the kitchen to let the disinfectants do their thing.

Not a lot to do, a couple of dirty plates.

–Espera a que abras el microwave –me dice Silvia, con esa sonrisa para adentro que le sale cuando se burla. Y sí, estaba realmente sucio. Manos a la obra. Estoy de lo más concentrado en mi faena cuando ella me dice:

–¡Mira!

Y desde la cama con una mano en alto muestra una foto de más de treinta años atrás. Una foto que he visto no sé cuántas veces. Y todavía la tiene, pensé.

Yo sigo limpiando. Ella sigue hablándome.

–En los setenta yo fui la primera. Éramos sólo cuatro locas en el magazine. Nos hacíamos un dineral. No había tanta competencia como ahora.

Termino con el microwave.

–Tienes que tapar la comida que calientas, mira que con el calor la comida salpica y se ensucia todo bien feo –le digo, como advirtiéndole para una próxima vez que venga a limpiar. Me tomo un vaso de agua. Vuelvo a terminar con el baño. Cepillo el inodoro y el lavamanos. Silvia continúa:

–Eso sí, yo nunca le robé a los pargos.

Respira profundo.

–Bueno, cuando no estaba en droga. Y tú lo sabes. Cuando una está en droga hace cualquier cosa.

Voy a la cocina por otro vaso de agua. Tengo el brazo cansado de tanto cepillar.

–Creo que todo está limpio.

«Just wait til you open the microwave,» Silvia tells me, with that sly smile she gets when she's making fun. Oh yes, it was really dirty. To work I go. I am completely absorbed in my labors when she shouts, «Look!»

And from the bed she sticks up her arm to show me a photo from over thirty years ago. A photo I've seen I don't know how many times. So she still has it, I think.

I keep cleaning. She keeps talking. «In the seventies I was the first. There was just us four locas in the magazine. We made a fortune. There wasn't as much competition as there is now.

I finish the microwave.

«You have to cover the food when you heat it up. Look how when it gets hot it splatters and gets it all dirty,» I tell her, like I'm letting her know for the next time I come to clean. I pause for a drink of water. I go back into the bathroom to finish up there. I brush the toilet and the sink. Silvia goes on.

«Though I never robbed from my johns.»

She breathes deeply.

«Well, when I wasn't on drugs anyway. And you know how it is. When you're on drugs you're capable of anything.»

I go to the kitchen for another glass of water. My arm is tired from scrubbing.

«I think everything's clean.»

Silvia mueve la cabeza en señal de aprobación. Me siento a la orilla de su cama.

–Oye Silvia, así que ya no te metes nada, ni yerba –le digo, mientras saco un pito de marihuana del bolsillo de mi pantalón.

–No, nada. Ya no me echo nada.

Yo prendo el pito y me doy como tres jalones. No más. Últimamente como que la mente ya no tiene el aguante de antes.

–Anyway, como que tú te quedaste en la misma nota forever –le digo, y nos ponemos a reír–. Anda, pásame los pies que te voy a dar un masaje.

Me los pasa. No puedo dejar de asombrarme.

–Oh, my god! ¡Hace cuánto que no te cortas las uñas de los pies!

–Ay, no me acuerdo. En el velador hay un cortaúñas. Cógelo.

Lo busco. Pulo como puedo esas uñas que parecen garras. Las calles han sido bien caminadas por estos pies, pienso. Los masajeo. Silvia conoce las calles de Nueva York sólo como las ratas lo hacen. Taco, taquito, tacón, Iris Chacón. Silvia tiene cara de felicidad después del masaje que le he dado.

–Loquita, me ultraboté –le digo.

Prendo de nuevo el pito de yerba. Silvia de pronto se pone de pie. Se sienta. Nuevamente se pone a hablar.

Silvia nods her approval. I sit on the edge of her bed.

«So Silvia, you really don't take anything anymore, not even weed?» I ask her as I take a joint out of my pocket.

«No, nothing. I don't take anything anymore.»

I light up the joint and take like three hits. No more than that. Lately it's like my mind can't take as much as it used to.

Anyway, just seems like you got high back then and now, well, you've just never, ever ever, come down,» I tell her, and we start to laugh. «OK give me your feet -- I'm going to give you a massage.»

She puts her feet up for me. I can't contain myself.

«Oh, my god! When was the last time you cut your nails?»

«Ay, I don't know. There's a set of clippers in the nightstand. See if you can find it.»

I go and get it. I file those nails, almost like claws, as best I can. The streets have been walked up and down by these feet, I think to myself. I massage them. The only ones who know the streets of New York better than Silvia are the rats. Click clack, she made the streets her own, like Iris Chacón. Silvia looks happy after the massage I've just given her.

«Loquita, I really went all out with that one -- all out,» I tell her.

–Yo no soy ninguna estúpida. He vivido en Nueva York todos estos años. Para que veas. Me han tirado de roofos. Tú sabes, uno de esos locos. Y para qué decir cuando me llegó ese tipo del magazine al departamento de la 44. El tipo sonaba bien nice. Blanco y todo.

Y me mira directo a los ojos.

–Tú sabes que yo nunca cogí ni morenos, ni latinos –continúa–. Pero para que veas: ese tipo me cañoneó. Me robó todo lo que había hecho ese día. No conforme con eso me dejó amarrada. Tuve que esperar más de diez horas así, hasta que llegara mi roommate. Si se demoraba un minute más me ponía a gritar por ayuda. No me iba a importar que tuvieran que tirar la puerta abajo y que me encontraran toda amarrada, con lencería y la peluca tirada en el piso. Qué bochorno.

Nos quedamos en silencio.

–Pero para que veas. He vivido todos estos años en Nueva York.

Me pongo de pie. Le pregunto dónde están los CD. Me responde qué quiero escuchar.

–Disco, of course.

Ella pone a Donna Summer y nos ponemos a bailar.

–Jamás tuve que hacer línea para entrar al Studio 54. Los guardias nos dejaban pasar de inmediato. Íbamos bien escandalosas y bellas.

I light up the joint again. Silvia gets up all of a sudden. She sits down. She starts talking again.

«I'm no fool. I've lived in New York all these years. You've got to understand. I've been slipped roofies. You know, by one of those crazies. What can I tell you –– when that guy from the magazine showed up to my apartment on 44th? He looked pretty nice. White and everything.»

And she looks me right in the eyes.

«You know I never went with black guys, or latinos,» she continues. «But just goes to show you. That guy pulled a gun on me. He stole everything I had made that day. And I guess that wasn't enough for him because he left me tied up. I had to wait more than ten hours like that, until my roommate showed up. If she had come more than a minute later I would have started screaming for help. I wouldn't have cared if they had to kick the door down and found me all tied up like that, in lingerie and with my wig thrown down on the ground. What a disgrace.»

We sit in silence a minute.

«Just goes to show. I've lived all these years in New York.»

I get up. I ask her where her CDs are. She asks me what I want to listen to.

«Disco, of course.»

She puts on Donna Summer and we start dancing.

«I never had to wait to get into Studio 54. The doormen let us right in. We were outrageous and beautiful.»

Nuevamente tiene la foto en la mano.

–Yo sí que anduve entre celebrities.

Se desploma en la cama. Yo sigo bailando. Me detengo. Me echo al lado de ella. Miramos el techo.

–Loquita, I had a lot of fun –me dice.

Y nos reímos a carcajadas. Nos quedamos en silencio. Me levanto. Ya tengo que irme. Silvia dice que me va a dejar a la salida. Le digo que no se preocupe, que descanse. Ella insiste. Tomamos el elevador y llegamos al lobby.

–Antes que te vayas, déjame mostrarte el comedor. Hoy hay bingo.

Y entramos a un cuarto amplio con varias mesas y sillas. Apenas cinco personas.

–No vino nadie –se queja una mujer.

–Te esperábamos –le dice otra a Silvia.

–Next week –responde ella, y me mira de reojo–. Ven.

Por el tono, y como la conozco bien, sé que me va a mostrar algo especial. Me lleva a una de las paredes del comedor. La pared tiene una cortina que va desde el techo hasta el suelo. Ella la levanta. Hay un estante que tiene algo parecido a pequeños jarrones en las repisas. No en todas. Algunas están vacías. Yo me quedo mirando a Silvia.

–Son las cenizas de la gente que ha vivido acá –me dice.

She holds up the photo again.

«I did hang around with celebrities.»

She falls down onto the bed. I go on dancing. I stop. I lay down next to her. We look up at the ceiling.

«Loquita, I had a lot of fun.»

And we bust out laughing. We lay quiet for a minute. I get up. I have to get going. Silvia says she'll walk me down. I tell her not to bother, she should just rest. She insists. The elevator takes us down to the lobby.

«Before you go, let me show you the dining room. Today they're having bingo.»

And we go into a big room with several tables and chairs. Not more than five people.

«Nobody came,» one woman complains.

«We were waiting for you,» another one tells Silvia.

«Next week,» she answers, and looks at me out of the corner of her eye. «Come.»

I know her well –– from the tone of her voice I know that she is going to show me something special. She takes me to one of the walls of the dining room. The wall has a curtain that goes from the ceiling to the floor. She raises it. There's a bookshelf that has something like little vases on the shelves. Not on all of them. Some of them are empty. I just look at Silvia.

«They're the ashes of the people who have lived here,» she tells me.

Me va a dejar a la puerta. Nos despedimos con un abrazo y un beso en la mejilla. Quedo de venir alguno de estos días, cuando se mejore el clima, para ir al parque. Caminando hacia el subway pienso que en realidad sí hubo gente para el bingo. Que el comedor estaba lleno, aunque la mayoría se retiró a descansar detrás de la cortina en la pared del comedor.

She walks me to the door. We say goodbye with a hug and a kiss on the cheek. I tell her I'll come back one of these days, when the weather gets better, and we'll go to the park. Walking to the subway I think to myself, there actually were people there for bingo. The dining room was full, even though most of them had stepped out to get some rest behind that curtain.

House of dreams

*Voy a hablar de un cuarto ubicado en la calle 46, entre
la Octava y Novena avenida. Manhattan. El cuarto
queda en un building que debe tener unos cien años,
en pleno restaurant Row Street. Se ubica en el tercer y
último piso, entre otros tres que comparten un baño.
Olvido decir que el building está entre un restaurant
ruso y otro chileno. El restaurant ruso es bien fancy
y, a pesar de que no lo conozco por dentro, desde fuera se pueden apreciar tres chandelier. Antes de ser un
restaurant eso era un edificio de pequeños apartamen-
tos. Así que para poder desocupar el lugar los rusos
tuvieron que ofrecer muy buenas sumas de dinero a
los que allí habitaban. Supe sólo de un anciano que se
resistía a marchar. Argumentaba que había vivido ahí
por muchos años junto a su esposa, ya fallecida, por lo
que el lugar estaba lleno de recuerdos. Y no hubo ma-
nera judicial de sacarlo de ahí. Así que a los rusos no
les quedó otra opción que hacerle un pequeño departamento dentro del fastuoso restaurant. Seguramente
este romántico anciano habrá pasado sus últimos años*

House of Dreams

I'm going to speak about a room located on 46th St., between Eighth Avenue and Ninth. Manhattan. The room is in a building that must be a hundred years old, right on Restaurant Row. The room is on the third and top floor, between three others it shares a bath with. I forgot to say that the building is between a Russian restaurant and a Chilean one. The Russian restaurant is pretty fancy. Although I've never been inside, from the street you can make out its three chandeliers. Before being a restaurant it was a building of small apartments. So in order to clear out the building the Russians had to offer really good sums of money to the people living there. I only heard of one old man who held out. He maintained that he had lived there for many years with his late wife, so the place was full of memories. And there was no legal way to get him out of there. So the Russians had no choice but to make a little apartment for him right there within the sumptuous restaurant. The romantic old man probably spent the last years of

bebiendo vodka y comiendo caviar junto al fantasma de su esposa.

A la izquierda del building está el restaurant chileno, del que puedo decir que fui una sola vez. La dueña era una chilena bien mala onda, pues además de pagar el mínimo a los camareros se quedaba con sus propinas. Eso me pareció muy desagradable, así que no volví. Su mala onda me hizo recordar a Chile, y de ahí a Pinochet. Quizás todo lo que sea mala onda y que venga de Chile me hace pensar en Pinochet. Pero volvamos al tercer piso del building, donde decía que el cuarto en cuestión compartía con otros tres, y un baño. Quienes habitaban ese tercer piso eran cuatro travestis. En el primer cuarto, una travesti mexicana, al igual que en el segundo. En el tercero, una travesti colombiana. Y la travesti de nuestro cuarto era de Argentina y se llamaba Francesca. Pero aún no diré nada de ella, sino que pasaré a describir el lugar. El cuarto había sido redecorado en todos sus aspectos, tanto que uno se olvidaba que ahí había vivido una travesti chilena que, por dedicarse a fumar crack, ya no había podido pagar la renta; así que ese mal clon de la Bolocco le dejó el cuarto a la que en ese entonces era su vecina, Francesca, la argentina. Ésta hizo posesión del lugar vacío como cuando Chile le cedió parte de la Patagonia a la Argentina. Y volcó toda su imaginación en decorar su nuevo hábitat. Lo transformó en

his life drinking vodka and eating caviar next to his wife's ghost.

To the left of the building is the Chilean restaurant, that I can say I went to exactly once. The owner was a Chilean woman who was pretty mala onda –– in addition to only paying the waiters minimum wage, she kept their tips. That seemed awful to me, so I never went back. Her mala onda reminded me of Chile, and of Pinochet. Maybe everything mala onda coming out of Chile reminds me of Pinochet. But let's get back to the third floor of the building, where I was saying that the room in question shared a bathroom with three other rooms. The inhabitants of this third floor were four travestis. In the first room a Mexican. In the second room, same. In the third, a Colombian one. And the one in our room was from Argentina. Her name was Francesca. But I won't say anything about her yet; I'll describe the place first. The room had been redecorated in every sense, so much so that you couldn't tell that its previous occupant had been a Chilean travesti whose dedication to crack had kept her from paying the rent. At all. So this failed clone of Cecilia Bolocco left the room to her then-neighbor, Francesca the Argentinian. Francesca extended her control over the empty territory just like when Chile ceded part of Patagonia to Argentina. And she poured all her creativity into decorating her new habitat. She

un cuarto hermosamente kitsch, donde abundaba el plateado, el dorado y el blanco de las paredes. Muchos espejos y, en un rincón de la cama, que era un colchón en el suelo, rodeado de satín celeste y transparencias, una pequeña mesa que simulaba un bar, donde lo que nunca faltaba era el vodka, el Bacardí y el tequila. Sobre una cómoda pintada de blanco y dorado había una pequeña imagen del buda feliz para la abundancia y la buena suerte, rodeado de billetes de un dólar y uno que otro de cinco y de diez. Francesca nunca quiso poner billetes de veinte, pues siempre desaparecían: nam miojo rengue kio, nam riojo rengue kio. Recuerdo que en la última navidad Francesca puso sobre la cama una muñeca Barbie que no tenía más nombre que el de Barbie. Así que cuando se visitaba a la dueña de casa –en este caso, de cuarto– era requisito obligatorio, aparte de saludar al buda, saludar a la muñeca en cuestión. En las paredes abundaban espejos, fotos de Francesca y de algunos novios que nunca fueron presentados, más una que otra boas de plumas en naranja, pink o azul eléctrico. También había una pequeña cocina con todo lo indispensable para las hambrientas amigas que siempre la visitaban. Francesca reemplazó las viejas alfombras por un piso plástico que simulaba ser de madera, más fácil de limpiar y más higiénico; esas alfombras agarraban mucha basura, desde lo que vuelcan los vasos en

transformed it into a room that was beautifully kitsch, with an overabundance of silver, gold, and white on the walls. Lots of mirrors, and at one corner of the bed (which was a mattress on the floor with a light blue and sheer satin bed skirt) there was a little table doubling as a bar where the vodka, Bacardi, and tequila always flowed freely. On top of a dresser painted white and gold there was a little image of the happy Buddha of good luck and abundance surrounded by one-dollar bills (with a couple of fives and tens thrown in). Francesca never wanted to put twenties there because they had a way of disappearing: nam mioho renge kyo, nam mioho renge kyo. I remember last Christmas when Francesca lay on the bed a Barbie doll who we just called Barbie. So when you paid a visit to the lady of the house, or room as the case may be, you were required to pay your respects not only to the Buddha but also to the doll. The walls overflowed with mirrors, photos of Francesca and a few boyfriends we were never introduced to in person, and a few orange, pink, and electric blue feather boas. There was also a small kitchen with everything she needed to feed the various hungry friends who were always popping over. Francesca replaced the carpet with faux wood plastic flooring, easier to clean and more hygienic; those rugs held on to a lot -- from whatever spilled out of cocktail glasses on drunken nights, to various other fluids. One

noches de embriaguez a fluidos varios. Un elemento importante: cuando entrabas, al lado izquierdo había una cortina negra que caía desde el techo, dividiendo el espacio en dos, como si fuera un telón que al abrirse mostraba una escenografía en la más Toulouse Lautrec. Era un lugar absolutamente acogedor, en especial para esos inviernos neoyorkinos que se hacen tan largos. Por ahí pasaba todo el mundo. Especialmente después de medianoche, cuando el business comenzaba. Hombres bellos, hombres feos, hombres pequeños, hombres altos, hombres negros, hombres blancos; eso sí, todos hombres con dinero, pues nuestra querida Francesca era una artista completa, de todo servicio, en el más occidental significado que puede tener la palabra geisha. Debo agregar que en alguna de esas tantas noches de visitas varoniles uno de ellos, después de realizados todos los ritos, reaccionó en forma violenta. Sicopática, che, diría Francesca. El tipo hizo pedazos la mesita del bar, que estaba toda tapizada en espejo, y que fue reemplazada por una más folklórica pintada de plateado. El loco en cuestión reaccionó como muchos de ellos que están en el clóset y no quieren admitir que sienten esos deseos libidinosos. Lo importante es que a nuestra argentina amiga no le pasó nada, y su suerte fue distinta a la de otras que ya descansan sobre nubes de colores en algún lugar de este universo. A veces pienso en el cuarto de Francesca

more thing: when you came in, on the left-hand side there was a black drape hung from the ceiling that divided the space in two, as if it were a curtain that would open to reveal a stage set designed by Toulouse Lautrec. It was a totally welcoming space, especially for those New York winters that have a tendency to drag on. Absolutely everyone passed through there. Particularly after midnight, when business hours began. Handsome men, ugly men, short men, tall men, black men, white men, but all men with money -- our dear Francesca was a total artist, offering complete service, in the most western sense of the word «geisha.» I should add that on one of these nights of manly visitors, there was one of them who, after finishing everything he had come there to finish, had a violent reaction. «Psychotic, che,» as Francesca would say. The guy destroyed the little bar-table, which was covered in mirror tiles, and which was later replaced by a more artisanal one painted silver. The psychotic reacted like many closeted men who don't want to admit they feel those libidinous desires. But the important thing is that our Argentinian friend was not hurt, and her fate was no different from that of so many others who are now resting on colored clouds some place in this universe. Sometimes I think of Francesca's room like a nightclub. A neon blue *nightclub* where all the dresses are covered

como un night club. Un night club en azul neón con vestidos saturados de lentejuelas. Como alguna vedette del sur de Sudamérica, Antártica, y con mucho brillo, ¿cachái? Me acuerdo de la Fresia Soto con lentes de contacto verdes cantando «Corazón, de melón, de melonmelonmelonmelonmelón, corazón». Esta vedette chilena era bien diferente a la Susana Giménez, la ídola de Francesca. Pero no sé por qué me acuerdo de la Fresia Soto, ya que Susana y Francesca son rubias, de ese platinado que sólo lo artificial puede dar.

Desde este cuarto nunca se sabía si afuera era de noche o de día, como en los after hour. Salud, cheers, salud. Larga vida a la noche y a los dinerales que pueda traer. Cuando Francesca no estaba el cuarto era atendido –o, mejor dicho, el teléfono era contestado– por Lorena, también conocida como Hugo Loren, quien había dejado Chile muchos años atrás. Era toda una mujer. A pesar de que hace años se había sacado los senos de silicón y se veía como un señor, todos la llamábamos Lorena. Por concretar las citas recibía muy buen pago en diosa blanca y, aunque esa diosa la había enviado más de una docena de veces al hospital, a ella no le importaba. Decía que ya había enterrado a tantas, y que aún le quedaban muchas más por enterrar, a propósito de ese humor negro que nos ha servido para soportar más de un amargo momento. Así se sentía nuestra querida Francesca en

in sequins. Like some showgirl from southernmost South America, the Antarctic, with lots of dazzle, you know what I mean? I remember Fresia Soto wearing green contacts and singing «Corazón, de melón, de melonmelonmelonmelonmelón, corazón.» This Chilean showgirl was different from Susana Giménez, Francesca's idol. So I don't know why I'm reminded of Fresia Soto, especially since both Francesca and Susana are blondes, the kind of platinum blond you can only get with the really artificial dyes.

When you were in this room you could never tell if it was day or night out, like in an after-hours. Cheers, salud, cheers. Long live the night and the fortunes it might bring. When Francesca was not home, the room was minded -- or rather, the phone was answered -- by Lorena, also known as Hugo Loren, who had left Chile many years before. A total woman. Despite the fact that a few years ago she had removed her silicone breasts and she looked like a man, we all called her Lorena. In exchange for arranging dates, she was paid handsomely in White Lady. The same White Lady had already sent her to the hospital over a dozen times, but she didn't care. She said that she had already buried so many, and that there were still so many left for her to bury. That sense of black humor got us through many a bitter moment. That's how Francesca felt on

más de alguna ocasión: I'm a pin up girl, decía. Una chica de calendario, de un calendario con muchos días festivos.

Uno de sus últimos tragos favoritos se llamaba Marilyn, y la persona que le enseñó a prepararlo contó que llevaba ese nombre por lo de aquella actriz trágica hollywoodense, que lo había hecho su favorito. Incluso se comentaba que era lo que había bebido antes de ir a cantarle el happy birthday a Kennedy en el Madison Square Garden. El trago en cuestión es un shot de vodka, Absolut por supuesto, que es bien magazine, y el resto de champagne. Así que ya se imaginarán qué pasaba cuando se bebía más de un par de copas: Marilyn se poseía de Francesca y viceversa. La noche suavemente empezaba a verse en tigre. Y ese cuarto era una cápsula desde donde se salía directo a un taxi amarillo que nos llevaba a una barra absolutamente plástica.

Ahí todos los días era fin de semana. Todo, una burbuja de placeres. Una burbuja que albergaba los siete pecados capitales. Una burbuja que se infló e infló hasta que reventó.

more than one occasion: «I'm a pin-up girl,» she would say. A calendar girl. On a calendar with lots of holidays.

One of her favorite cocktails was called the Marilyn, and the person who taught her how to make it told her that it was named after that tragic Hollywood actress, who had made it a favorite. They even said that it was what she had drunk before going to sing happy birthday to Kennedy in Madison Square Garden. The drink in question is a shot of vodka (Absolut of course, which is so magazine) and then the rest champagne. So you can imagine what happened when Francesca drank a few Marilyns: Francesca became possessed by Marilyn and vice versa. The night gradually got more and more violent. And that room became an escape pod from which we could exit into a yellow taxi that would take us to a totally plastic bar.

There, every day was a weekend. Everything was a bubble of pleasure. A bubble that held all seven mortal sins. A bubble that swelled and swelled until it burst.

Lo que necesito es dinero

Charlotte estaba de lo más enamorada. No recordaba bien cuándo lo había conocido, seguramente algún sábado por la noche. Apenas lo había visto entrar a la barra, hace un par de meses, le había comentado a Ivonne, la bartender:

–Mira ese tipo que va entrando. Me gusta.

–Ay, chulita. No es mi tipo –le había replicado la mexicana de ensiliconado rostro.

Era un tipo alto, joven, de contextura atlética; pero no era eso lo que a ella le había llamado la atención, sino más bien ese cabello con gel y anteojos de frame metálico en ese rostro de hombre bello. El bombón en cuestión se sentó en un lugar algo distante de ella. Mal comienzo, pues Charlotte era un poco tímida cuando se trataba de dar el primer paso, demasiado como para coquetearle y hacer que se sentara algo más cerca de ella. Así que se acordó de lo que alguna vez su hermana le había comentado acerca de las energías sicotrónicas, que eran algo así como enviar energías desde la mente para que la persona elegida pusiera inmediata atención en uno. Y al

What I Need Is Money

Charlotte couldn't be more in love. She couldn't remember when she had met him, must have been one Saturday night. As soon as she saw him come into the bar, a couple of months ago, she'd told the bartender Ivonne, «Look at that guy coming in now. I like him.»

«Ay, chulita. He's not my type,» replied the Mexican with her face of silicone.

He was a tall guy, young, with an athletic build. But that was not what had caught her attention; it was that slicked-back hair and metallic-framed glasses on that handsome man's face. The bombón in question sat down on a stool kind of far from her. Bad start, since Charlotte was a little shy when it came to making the first move, too shy to flirt with him and make him sit a little closer to her. So she remembered what her sister had once told her about psychotronic energies, which were something like energies you could send out from your mind so that the chosen person would immediately notice you.

parecer Charlotte era una experta en eso de las energías sicotrónicas, pues no pasaron ni cinco minutos para que las susodichas energías trabajaran y consiguieran que esta especie de Clark Kent se sentara a su lado. Charlotte lo mira de reojo. Él pide una cerveza. Mientras se la sirven, la bartender le susurra a Charlotte:

–Pero qué poder, chulita.

Charlotte gira un poco la cabeza. Lo mira directo a los ojos y le dice:

–Are you having fun?

Y él la mira y le sonríe sin contestar.

Ella repite:

–Are you having fun?

Hasta que él contesta con un remedo a lo robot:

–Are. U. Ha. Ving. Fun?

Y no es que Charlotte piense que el tipo es un robot, sino que después tantos años viviendo en Nueva York y escuchando inglés con tan diferentes acentos, supo de inmediato que el chico este es extranjero, y que obviamente no habla muy bien inglés. Así que le sonríe y le dice:

–Where're you from?

Él contesta con una amplia sonrisa, como si fuera una pregunta a la que ya estuviera acostumbrado.

–Poland.

–Oh! So you are Polish.

Y a ella eso le gusta. Alguien de aquellas tierras lejanas donde debe hacer mucho frío, mucha lluvia y mucho

And Charlotte was seemingly an expert in these psychotronic energies, because not even five minutes had gone by before the said energies took effect and got this Clark Kent to sit down next to her. Charlotte looked at him out of the corner of her eye. He orders a beer. As they serve it to him, the bartender whispers to Charlotte, «What powers you have, chulita.»

Charlotte turns her head slightly. She looks at him right in the eyes and says, «Are you having fun?»

He looks at her and smiles but does not answer.

She repeats, «Are you having fun?»

Finally he repeats after her like a robot, «Are. U. Ha. Ving. Fun?»

It's not that Charlotte thinks this guy is a robot, just that after so many years living in New York and listening to English spoken in such different accents, she knew right away that this boy is a foreigner, and that he obviously doesn't speak English very well. So she smiles at him and says, «Where're you from?»

He answers with a big smile, as if it were a question he were used to answering. «Poland.»

«Oh! So you are Polish.»

She likes that. Someone from those faraway lands where it must be so cold, so rainy, and so green. Autumn afternoons looking at the trees out

verde. *Tardes otoñales mirando los árboles desde alguna ventana. Pues esa onda como de Europa del Este a Char-lotte la pone en estado romántico. Y, sumándole ese acen-to tan marcado al hablar, eso hizo que nuestra amiga se encendiera y le tomara esas manos grandes para posarlas en ese miembro suyo que esa noche se escondía bajo unas panty hose de color off black. Charlotte se le acerca.*

–Can you invite me a drink?

Porque a ella, aunque diera el look de dama, no le iba eso de esperar a que la invitaran. Y el polaco como pensando, más bien como traduciendo lo que ella dice, pasados algunos segundos responde:

–Of course. What you want?

–Red label on the rocks.

En la barra todo está a oscuras. Pero entre los co-mensales se pueden distinguir muy bien los rostros, gatos que saben ver de noche.

Charlotte ya tenía su scotch. Se toma casi todo de un solo trago. Luego mueve coquetamente la cabeza con su nueva peluca negra estilo Betty Boop y dice, haciendo crujir pedacitos de hielo entre los dientes:

–Let's go upstairs.

Y él la sigue al segundo piso, donde es más privado. Allí se sientan muy juntitos en un sofá. Comienzan a besarse. Ella le retira los anteojos, haciendo esa cara más hermosa a causa de la excitación. Le desordena algo ese cabello peinado con gel. Lo mira detenidamente

some window. The whole Eastern Europe thing got Charlotte in a romantic mood. Add that noticeable accent, and our friend Charlotte got all worked up and could not help but take those big hands of his and put them on the bulge she was hiding that night under some off-black pantyhose. Charlotte leans in.

«Can you invite me a drink?»

Because, although she was looking very ladylike that night, she wasn't down with the whole waiting around until he invites you thing. And the Polish guy sits a few seconds thinking, or more likely translating what she has just said, and then answers, «Of course. What you want?»

«Red Label on the rocks.»

In the bar everything is on dim. But you can make out the faces of the patrons, cats who can see in the dark.

Now Charlotte had her scotch. She drinks it down almost in one gulp. Then she coquettishly moves her head with her new Betty Boop-style black wig and, crushing bits of ice between her teeth, says, «Let's go upstairs.»

So he follows her to the second floor, where it's more private. They sit right up next to each other on a couch. They start to kiss. She takes off his glasses, his face looking even more beautiful as his blood starts rushing. She musses his gelled hair. She gives him a

mientras lo besa. Y entre tanta pasión de pronto Char-
lotte se acuerda. No es que se hubiera olvidado, ya que
siempre lo tiene presente: esta noche, como todas las
noches, ha venido a la barra a buscar dinero. Así que
le pregunta a su chico de turno:

–Do you have a tip for me?

Y el polaco, tomándose más de varios segundos
para contestar y antes de poner a Charlotte más ner-
viosa de lo que ya estaba, le dice:

–How much?

Nuestra amiga, ya un poco aliviada, le contesta:

–How much you have?

–Forty is ok?

Y ella se los agarra de las manos apenas los está
sacando de la billetera. Claro, cuarenta son cuarenta,
y además solo ha sido un lap dance con alguien que
para nada ha sido un esfuerzo, como cuando tocan
esos viejos repulsivos. Charlotte, que lo ha seguido be-
sando, se pone de pie y deja la pelvis cerca de la cara de
su amorcito polaco. Él juega con su lengua, pasándola
por ese miembro de mujer nocturna. Un miembro que
poco a poco va entrando en su boca. Pero Charlotte,
muy excitada y todo, no quiere venirse así como así.
Se vuelve a sentar junto a él, recuerda que ha venido a
lo que ha venido y le pregunta:

–Can you give me another tip?

Y él se queda repitiendo la palabra:

good hard look as she kisses him. And in the middle of all this passion suddenly Charlotte remembers. Not that she had forgotten, since it's always on her mind: this night, like all other nights, she has come to the bar to look for money. So she asks tonight's boy, «Do you have a tip for me?»

And the Polish guy, taking more than a few seconds to answer but before Charlotte could get more nervous than she already was, says, «How much?»

Our friend, a little relieved, answers him, «How much you have?»

«Forty is OK?»

And she grabs it from his hands as soon as he takes it from his wallet. Obviously, forty is forty, and plus it's just one lap dance with someone that didn't make it a chore like it is when she gets one of those repulsive older guys. Charlotte, who hasn't stopped kissing him, stands up and leaves her pelvis near the face of her new Polish amorcito. He plays with his tongue, moving it over the lady of the night's erect member. A member that finds its way into his mouth, bit by bit. But Charlotte, even as turned on as she is, doesn't want to come just like that. She sits back down next to him, remembers what she came there for, and asks him, «Can you give me another tip?»

He just repeats the word, «Tip. Tip. Tip.»

–Tip. Tip. Tip.

–Come on! You know what I mean –lo increpa Charlotte, algo impaciente.

Y como él le explica –o, más bien, es lo que ella entiende– que sólo le queda dinero para regresarse a Brooklyn, sin especificar si en subway o en taxi, se levanta pensando que por ahora cuarenta está bien, y que aún le quedan un par de horas para llenar su cartera. Así que lo besa apasionadamente, como para que se acuerda de ella y le dice:

–See you next time.

Y el polaco se queda ahí, todo excitado, mientras Charlotte baja las escaleras para buscar un nuevo amorcito. Y allí siguió nuestra amiga, todas las noches en la misma barra. Noches buenas, noches malas, pero siempre haciendo algo de dinero. Mantenía al polaco en su mente con eso de que quizás lo volviera a ver. Y así pasaron meses, que se sienten como un par de semanas en esta ciudad tan vertiginosa.

Charlotte se prepara con Ivanka, su amiga peruana, para ir a la fiesta de una tal Alana Star. Se trata de una actriz transexual porno que hace unas fiestas que dicen son un escándalo. Dicen, pues ni Charlotte ni Ivanka han asistido hasta ahora, hasta esa noche en que las dos ante el espejo se están maquillando.

–Charlotte, en las fiestas de Alana hay clientes de dinerales –comenta Ivanka.

«Come on! You know what I mean,» Charlotte insists, a little impatient.

And since he explains to her, or rather, as she understands him to say, he has just enough money left to get back to Brooklyn (though he doesn't specify whether he means by subway or taxi) she gets up thinking that forty is fine for now, and that she still has a couple of hours to fill her purse. So she kisses him passionately, so he won't forget her, and tells him, «See you next time.»

So the Polish guy is left there, all worked up, while Charlotte goes down the stairs to look for a new amorcito. And so our friend went on like this, every night at the same bar. Good nights, bad nights, but always making some money. She kept the Polish guy in her head –– you never know, maybe she could run into him again one day. Months went by, though they feel like weeks in this dizzying city.

Charlotte is getting ready with Ivanka, her Peruvian friend, to go to a party thrown by someone named Alana Star. She's a transsexual porn star who throws parties that apparently are a total escándalo. Apparently, because neither Charlotte nor Ivanka has been so far, until tonight when the two of them are making themselves up in the same mirror.

«Charlotte, at Alana's parties there are clients who are worth a fortune,» Ivanka informs her.

Charlotte esta noche se ha puesto una peluca corta de rubio casi platinado, y está enfajada con un negro corset sobre un vestido de encajes en color palo de rosa. Todo esto lo acompaña de unos correspondientes high heels transparentes. Ivanka va más discreta, no tan travesti como Charlotte. Y es que la peruana ya iba en la onda de hacerse el cambio de sexo, así que trataba de pasar unspookable. Vivía de mujer las veinticuatro horas, los siete días a la semana. Charlotte estaba algo preocupada, pues le habían dicho que pedían identificación para entrar al lugar y ella no tenía ni siquiera una de esa falsas.

–Tú sabes, Ivanka. Ahora piden identificación por todo.

–Por culpa de esos terroristas, pues, Charlotte. Mira que lo de las torres no fue ningún chiste.

Pero esas preocupaciones sólo fueron un gasto de energía, porque las dos entraron como si nada al party. Jamás les preguntaron por identificación.

–Te lo dije. Aquí las locas somos las reinas. Mmm, bueno: quiero decir ustedes las dragas, pues yo soy una mujer.

La fiesta se realizaba en una discotheque en Midtown Manhattan. Era un lugar bien amplio con una barra al principio y otra al final. En el medio se ubicaba un pequeño stage, donde algunas chicas mostraban en todo su esplendor los últimos adelantos en cirugía plástica. Si antes, en las fiestas de los ochenta, debías

Tonight Charlotte has put on a short blonde –– almost platinum –– wig, and she's tied into a black corset over top a rosewood-colored lace dress. And of course the obligatory transparent high heels. Ivanka is looking more discreet, not as travesti as Charlotte. Because our Peruvian was already all about the sex change, so she was trying to go unspookable. She lived as a woman twenty-four hours a day, seven days a week. Charlotte was a little worried because she had heard they asked for ID to get into this place, and she didn't have any, not even a fake one.

«You know, Ivanka. Now they ask for ID everywhere.»

«It's all the fault of those terrorists, Charlotte. The Twin Towers thing was no joke.»

But those worries were just a waste of energy, because they let both of them into the party just like that. They never asked them for ID.

«I told you. Around here locas rule. Well, I mean you drag queens do –– I am a woman.»

The party was being held in a dance club in Midtown Manhattan. It was a pretty big place with a bar at the beginning and another at the end. In the middle there was a small stage, where some of the girls showed off the latest advances in plastic surgery in all its glory. Before, in the eighties, you went to parties bragging

presumir de cuánto habías gastado en el gown de label, hoy en día se trata de mostrar cuánto has gastado en el cirujano plástico. Y algunas de tanto gastar se habían extralimitado con los resultados. El lugar estaba repleto de chicas que no se veían desde hace tiempo; aunque eso del tiempo era algo relativo, ya que apenas pasaban un par de semanas sin que una loca se viera por ahí ya la daban por presa, hospitalizada o deportada. Por lo menos para darla por muerta se esperaban algún tiempo más. Y ahí estaban todas: Cassandra, Erika, Ury, la Machete, Pamela, Cristina y hay que decir etcétera, etcétera, etcétera, pues eran muchas. Un aquelarre neoyorkino. Y para qué decir de los hombres que ahí andaban: todos clientes en potencia con una generosa billetera. Charlotte escuchó como uno de ellos exclamaba:

–I feel like a kid in a candy store!

Después de beber Ivanka su correspondiente glass of champagne y Charlotte su red label on the rocks, después de dos pases bien correctos de cocaína, se ponen a merodear cada una por su lado. Charlotte se para cerca del stage. Ahí, toda encantada con las chicas que bailan una música entre espacial y tecno, comienza a girar en busca de algún conocido que no sea una loca, sino un potencial cliente. Y apenas se da vuelta lo ve a él, al polaco. Lleva los mismos lentes de frame metálico y el cabello peinado con gel. Ella se le acerca y le dice:

about how much you had spent on a designer gown, but nowadays it's all about how much you spend on your surgeon. And some of the girls had spent so much they kind of went overboard. The place was stuffed to the gills with girls who had not seen each other in a long time. Although, time was a very relative thing, since it only took a few weeks of a loca not showing her face for everyone to assume she had been arrested, hospitalized, or deported. At least though, to assume she was dead they waited a little while longer. Everyone was there: Cassandra, Erika, Ury, la Machete, Pamela, Cristina, and well, you just have to say etcetera, etcetera, etcetera, because there were so many of them. A real New York coven. And what can you say about the men walking around: all potential clients with generous wallets. Charlotte heard one of them exclaim, «I feel like a kid in a candy store!»

After Ivanka drank her usual glass of champagne and Charlotte her Red Label on the rocks, and after two good bumps of cocaine, each of them starts to roam around on her own. Charlotte stops near the stage. There, loving the sight of all the girls dancing to that mix of space and techno, she starts to make the rounds in search of some friendly face that wasn't another loca but a potential client. And no sooner does she turn her head, but there he is, the Polish guy. He's wearing the same metallic-frame glasses and the gelled-back hair.

–Hi.

Luego le da la espalda, ya segura de que la ha reconocido a pesar del cambio de peluca. Ahí sigue mirando dragas que suben y bajan del stage, mientras flashes de fotógrafos las encandilan. Pues hay que decir que la fiesta era una producción a todo dar. Todas son famosas en sus quince segundos, ya ni siquiera quince minutos como la Warhol. De pronto Charlotte siente cómo una mano le toca esa cintura creada a puro apretuje de corset. Luego siente cómo le acarician la espalda. Ya no aguanta más. Sabe que es el polaco. Gira y comienza a besarlo. Se besan y todo da vueltas alrededor de ellos. Charlotte lo lleva a unos sofás que se ubican cerca de la barra que está en la parte de atrás. Se sientan y siguen besándose. Pasa Ivanka, irónica.

–Pero Charlotte, parece que te has enamorado –le dice, y con una seña la invita al baño. Charlotte sabe que eso significa unos pases de cocaína, que por ahorita no caerían nada de mal. Le dice al polaco que la espere, que por mientras le pida un red label on the rocks. Una vez dentro del baño, metidas en una cabina de toilet y dándose sus ansiados sniffs, Ivanka, que conoce bien a Charlotte, la aconseja:

–Oye, nada de enamorarse, que hay que trabajar.

Posando ante el espejo, las dos de pronto se quedan como atrapadas por el reflejo. Ivanka se pasa las yemas

120

She comes up to him and says, «Hi.»

Then she turns her back, assured he has recognized her despite the new wig. She goes on looking at the drag queens getting on stage and coming back down, as camera flashes illuminate them. Because it must be said, this party was a huge production. Everyone had her fifteen seconds of fame –– not even fifteen minutes like la Warhol said. Suddenly Charlotte feels a hand touching the waist she had created by tightening her corset. Then she feels someone rubbing her back. She can't stand it any more. She knows it's the Polish guy. She turns around and starts kissing him. They kiss and everything whirls around them. Charlotte takes him off to some couches placed near the bar in back. They sit down and go on kissing.

Ivanka walks by, ironically. «Well well well, Charlotte. Looks like you're in love.» And she motions for Charlotte to join her in the bathroom. Charlotte knows this means a couple bumps of cocaine, which wouldn't feel too bad right about now. She tells the Polish guy to wait right there, and to order her a Red Label on the rocks for when she gets back. Once they're in the bathroom closed up in a stall and taking greedy sniffs, Ivanka, who knows Charlotte all too well, gives her some advice:

«Look –– none of this falling in love business. We're here to work.» Posing in the mirror, the two of them get caught up in their own reflection. Ivanka

de los dedos, dándose pequeños golpecitos en todo el rostro como revisando que la estructura de su cara está en su lugar. Charlotte se concentra en la boca, ya que después de tanto besuqueo con el polaco, el lipstick rojo se le ha salido del dibujo de los labios; luce igual que un niño cuando se toma un helado de fresa. Se retoca la boca para dejarla nuevamente en la cosa corazón de paloma.

–Cómo tendrá la boca el tipo con él te estas besando –agrega Ivanka, con esa risa tan poco melodiosa que le da cuando se embala.

Charlotte toma un trozo de papel de baño y sale directo a los labios del polaco, para limpiarlo de todo vestigio de lápiz labial. De un solo trago se toma casi todo su red label on the rocks. Y comienza besarlo de nuevo. La música está bien fuerte. Como corresponde. La gente, toda en nota de haber consumido algo. Casi nadie baila. Solo las dragas que están en el stage; aunque en realidad tampoco bailan, más bien lo que hacen es mover los implantes de agua salina y las caderas pompeadas de silicón. La cosa J. Lo. Pero Charlotte, que anda en la onda de divertirse, levanta al polaco del sofá y lo lleva al centro del lugar. Y así, bailando y besándose, Charlotte se acuerda de lo que Ivanka le había dicho en el baño:

–Nada de enamorarse, que hay que trabajar.

Así que acerca sus labios a los oídos de su enamorado y, susurrando, le dice:

gives herself little taps with her fingertips, all over her face, as if checking to make sure her facial structure was all set in the right place. Charlotte concentrates on her mouth, since after making out with the Polish guy her red lipstick has smudged outside her lip-line; she looks just like a kid who just ate strawberry ice cream. She retouches her lipstick to get that dove-heart effect. «What must his mouth look like, the guy you've been making out with,» adds Ivanka, laughing that unmelodious laugh that she gets when she's tripping.

Charlotte takes a piece of toilet paper and goes out straight to the Polish guy's lips, to clean off any trace of lipstick. In one swig she drinks almost all her Red Label on the rocks. And she starts to kiss him again. The music is really loud. As it should be. The people, all high from one thing or another. Hardly anyone is dancing. Only the drag queens that are up on stage; though actually they're not really dancing either. What they're doing is moving around their saline implants and their hips pumped full of silicone. The whole J-Lo thing. But Charlotte, who's all about having fun tonight, picks the Polish guy up off the couch and takes him to the center of the place. And there, dancing and kissing him, Charlotte remembers what Ivanka told her in the bathroom:

«None of this falling in love business. We're here to work.» So she puts her lips up against her love's ears, and whispers to him, «Do you have a tip for me?»

–*Do you have a tip for me?*

Y él, automáticamente y sin hablar, a lo robot le da tres billetes de veinte dólares que ella guarda en su cartera roja de charol Donna Karan, regalada por una amiga años atrás para una navidad, una tal Francesca, poco antes de que se volviera loca, de que se perdiera en medio de Times Square, tragada por esta gran urbe como muchas otras. A veces le bajaba esa nota a Charlotte de acordarse en los momentos más inesperados de alguna amiga que ya no estaba. Y le daba por verlas sentadas en la barra, como con ganas de ir a comentarles algo. Pero esos pensamientos duraban sólo unos segundos. Aparecían y desaparecían como un flash. Le pide otro red label on the rocks al polaco. Él se lo va a comprar. Se lo trae. Le saca la t-shirt. Lo deja a torso desnudo. Siguen bailando. Llega Ivanka y le habla:

–*Nos vamos, Charlotte. Me llevo un pargo que nos va a dar un ride. Anda manejando.*

Charlotte le responde que ella se va a llevar al polaco. Ivanka la increpa:

–*Te va a pagar?*

–*Of course!* –*se defiende Charlotte.*

Inmediatamente se pega al oído del polaco:

–*You have a tip for go to my home?*

–*Other sixty* –*contesta él.*

124

He, automatically and without saying anything, robot-style, gives her three twenty-dollar bills which she puts away in her Donna Karan red patent leather purse, given to her as a Christmas present years ago by a friend, a certain Francesca, shortly before she went crazy and got lost in the middle of Times Square, swallowed up by this great city like so many others have been. Once in a while Charlotte got herself down remembering, at the most unexpected moments, some good girlfriend who was not around anymore. And she would see them all sitting at the bar, as if she really wanted to go tell them something. But those thoughts would only last a few seconds. They would appear and disappear as if in a flash. She asks the Polish guy to get her another Red Label on the rocks. He goes to get it for her. He brings it back. She takes his t-shirt off. She leaves him barechested. They keep on dancing.

Ivanka comes up to them and says, «We're leaving, Charlotte. I'm going with a trick who can give us a ride. He drives.» Charlotte answers that she was leaving with the Polish guy.

Ivanka needles her: «Is he going to pay you?»

«Of course!» Charlotte defends herself.

Immediately she's back up in the Polish guy's ear: «You have a tip for go to my home?»

«Other sixty,» he replies.

Charlotte lo agarra de un ala y sigue a Ivanka, que tiene el aventón. Salen directo a la calle. Y ya afuera a Charlotte le da la impresión de estar en una fortaleza de asfalto. Los tacones suenan fuertes y en eco. Claro, la nota, se dice Charlotte.

El cliente de Ivanka llega en una camioneta. Charlotte se instala atrás con su chico. Se van tocando. Llegan al departamento de Ivanka, que queda en el West Village. Ella se dirige a su dormitorio y Charlotte queda en la sala. Hacen y deshacen con el polaco. Se tenían ganas, así que la cosa es bien intensa. Aparece Ivanka y le cuenta que su pargo ya se va, así que es mejor que despache al suyo. Y como la casa es de Ivanka, Charlotte hace caso:

–Babe, you have to go.

Él, bien obediente, se comienza a vestir.

–Bye, babe.

Se besan y ella lo va a dejar a la puerta. Él se marcha. Ivanka viene de su cuarto con una bolsa de coca.

–Démonos otro pase.

Se sienta en el sofá.

–Huele a cacha.

Da un jale y le ofrece otro a Charlotte, que lo recibe mientras piensa en voz alta:

–Creo que me gusta. Y yo también le gusto.

Como que hubiese hecho un clic con la coca, Ivanka la interrumpe en tono imperativo:

126

Charlotte drags him away by one arm and follows Ivanka, who's getting the ride. They go out onto the street. Once outside, Charlotte feels like she's in an asphalt fortress. Her heels are loud and they echo. Oh right, I'm high, Charlotte reminds herself.

Ivanka's client arrives in a van. Charlotte seats herself in the back with her guy. They can't keep their hands off each other. They get to Ivanka's apartment, which is in the West Village. She goes to her bedroom and Charlotte stays in the living room. Charlotte and the Polish guy are all over each other in a thousand ways. They were hot for each other, so it gets pretty intense. Ivanka appears and tells her that her john is on his way out already, so she should get rid of hers too. And since it's Ivanka's house, Charlotte has to listen to her.

«Babe, you have to go.»

He starts to get dressed, obediently.

«Bye, babe.»

They kiss and she walks him to the door. He leaves. Ivanka comes back out of her room with a bag of blow.

«Let's do some more coke.» She sits down on the couch. «It smells like fucking in here.»

She does a bump and offers one to Charlotte, who is thinking out loud as she accepts it, «I think I like him. And he likes me.»

Ivanka interrupts her sternly, as if the coke had made something click in her:

–Charlotte: nada de enamorarse, que hay que pensar en el dinero.

Se fuman un cigarrillo. Están cansadas.

–Bueno, me voy a mi cuarto. Hablamos mañana.

Charlotte se queda en el sofá. Piensa en cuánto le gusta el polaco. Que el sexo es bueno. Que hacen de todo. Buena verga, pero con pellejo por delante, y es bello cuando se ve la cabeza de la verga, piensa. Pero no le importa, porque sabe que está a punto de enamorarse, así que eso de la verga no le llama mucho la atención. Así se duerme, pensando que tal vez ha encontrado novio.

Después de un par de horas el bulldog de Ivanka la despierta a puro ladrido. Igual cute el perro, parece de peluche. Y Charlotte, que es media niña para sus cosas, se pone a jugar con la mascota:

–I'm in love, 007. ¿Qué me dices? Parece que he encontrado boyfriend.

Su celular comienza a sonar. Es un número que ella desconoce.

–Hello? Yes.

Le comenta en voz baja al 007, el perro.

–Es él. ¡Me olvide que le había dado mi número!

Y 007, con las orejas bien paradas.

–Yes, babe. So you are at work. Okay. Okay. Eat something good for lunch. Yes, call me after work.

«Charlotte. None of this falling in love business. Keep your mind on the money.»

They smoke a cigarette. They are tired.

«Ok. I'm going to my room. Talk tomorrow.»

Charlotte stays on the couch. She thinks about how much she likes the Polish guy. How the sex is good. How they try everything. Nice cock, but with foreskin, and it's nice when you can see the head poking out, she thinks. But that doesn't really matter, because she knows she's about to fall in love, so she doesn't think about the foreskin thing that much. She falls asleep like this, thinking she may have found herself a boyfriend.

After a couple of hours Ivanka's bulldog wakes her up barking. The dog is cute though, almost looks like a stuffed animal. And Charlotte, who's like a little girl when it comes to things like this, starts playing with the pet.

«I'm in love, 007. How about that? Guess I've found myself a boyfriend.»

Her cell begins to ring. It's from an unknown number.

«Hello? Yes.»

She explains to 007, under her breath: «It's him. I forgot I'd given him my number!»

007's ears perk up.

«Yes, babe. So you are at work. Okay. Okay. Eat something good for lunch. Yes, call me after work.»

Deja el celular y se pone a jugar nuevamente con el 007, hasta que llega Ivanka desde su dormitorio.

–Me muero de hambre. Vamos a desayunar. No, mejor a almorzar de una vez, que ya es medio tarde.

Ivanka también se pone a jugar con el 007.

–Pero Charlotte, esa cara de felicidad. Parece que te hubieras hecho dinerales anoche.

Y Charlotte, mientras va al baño a darse una ducha, le va diciendo:

–Pues me he enamorado. El polaco va a ser mi boyfriend. Me acaba de llamar.

Mientras escucha correr la regadera, Ivanka le habla al perro:

–¿Por qué tu tía es tan tonta, 007? ¿Por qué, dime?

Se van a almorzar a un restaurant del hood. Las dos han trabajado, así que van a un restaurant italiano. Charlotte, que es golosa, se muere por un tiramisú. Ivanka ordena un caesar salad y Charlotte un penne pasta with pieces of grilled chicken and mushroom. Y así, comiendo, como que no quiere la cosa, Ivanka le da la onda reading a Charlotte:

–Ay, Charlotte. Así que estas enamorada.

–Creo que encontré a alguien nice. Además sabe lo que hago, y al parecer no le importa.

–Loca, sólo es un pargo. Y más encima, barato.

–No es feo. Al contrario, súper guapo

–Seguro. Que te dé dinero con su belleza.

She leaves the cell on the table and starts playing with 007 again, until Ivanka comes out of her room.

«I'm starving. Let's get some breakfast. No, actually let's just have lunch already, it's already kind of late.»

Ivanka gets down to play with 007 too.

«Charlotte, what's with that happy face? You look like you made a fortune last night.»

Charlotte tells her on her way to take a shower, «Well, I have fallen in love. The Polish guy is going to be my boyfriend. He just called me.»

Over the sound of the shower, Ivanka talks to her dog. «Why is your auntie so silly, 007? Tell me why.»

They go to get lunch at a restaurant in the hood. They both have been working, so they go to an Italian restaurant. Charlotte, the glutton, is dying for tiramisu. Ivanka orders a caesar salad and Charlotte a penne pasta with pieces of grilled chicken and mushroom. And while they eat, oh so casually, Ivanka gets down to reading Charlotte.

«Ay, Charlotte. So you're in love, huh.»

«I think I've found someone nice. Plus he knows what I do, and seems like it doesn't bother him.»

«Loca, he's just a trick. And a cheap one at that.»

«He's not ugly. Actually he's super handsome.»

«Right. Well I guess he can pay you with his looks.»

131

–Por qué siempre las locas tratan de tirarla a una para abajo –murmura Charlotte ante la insistencia de Ivanka–. Quedó de llamarme después del trabajo.

Ahora, más calmada, se llena la boca de pasta. Y así, con la boca llena, sigue:

–Aún no me conoce de día, pero él sabe que soy travesti y seguro que no le va a importar.

–Ahí tú, en tu nube. ¡Mientras no le haga daño a nadie! Tienes que pensar. ¿Acaso él te va a dar el dinero para que rentes tu cuarto?

Charlotte se queda medio inmovilizada.

–Tienes que pensar en ahorrar dinero.

–¿Acaso me estás sacando en cara que me estoy quedando en tu casa?

–Come on, relájate. Nada de eso. Te puedes quedar sin problemas en mi casa, pero no puedes estar pensando en novios cuando lo que necesitas es alguien que te resuelva.

Charlotte se queda pensando.

–Igual como que tienes razón.

Y cambian de tema. Ivanka ordena un capuchino y Charlotte un Earl Grey tea con su ansiado tiramisú. Dejan diez dólares de propina. Vuelven al departamento. Ivanka se queda limpiando y Charlotte saca a pasear al 007. Lo lleva por ahí. Mientras camina va pensando en todo el dinero que ha gastado en droga. Que no es capaz de juntar aunque sea quinientos dólares para rentarse

«How come these locas always feel the need to put me down,» Charlotte mumbles against Ivanka's persistence. «He promised to call me after work.»

Now, calmed down a little, she takes a mouthful of pasta. She keeps talking with her mouth full.

«He still hasn't seen me in the daytime but he knows I'm a travesti and I know he won't care.»

«Well just stay up there in the clouds then. As long as he doesn't hurt anyone. Keep your wits about you. You think he's going to give you the money to pay your rent?»

Charlotte sits there, almost paralyzed. «You need to think about saving up some money.»

«So now you're throwing it in my face that I'm staying at your house?»

«Oh relax. Nothing like that. You can stay with me, no problem. But you can't be there thinking about boyfriends when what you need is someone who can pay your bills.»

Charlotte sits there, thinking. «Maybe you're right.»

They change the subject. Ivanka orders a capuccino and Charlotte an Earl Grey tea with her coveted tiramisu. They leave a ten-dollar tip. They go back to the apartment. Ivanka stays to clean and Charlotte takes 007 out for a walk. As she walks she thinks about all the money she's spent on drugs. So she can't save even five hundred dollars to rent a room in Uptown

un cuarto Uptown Manhattan, donde se encuentran el mismo día. Con quinientos podría pagar un mes entero. Pero no. Se ha gastado eso y mucho más en droga.

–Así es la vida, 007.

Y el perro levanta la cabeza, la mira.

Charlotte vuelve donde Ivanka, deja al 007 y se va a buscar condones a centros comunitarios, centros de prueba del VIH, al Gay Center. Vende bolsas de cien condones por veinte dólares. Se los vende a las locas que tienen clientes en sus casas, que no van a las barras a buscar dinero. Ponen avisos en los periódicos y en un website que recién ha aparecido: Transexual Escort Services. Hace unas cuantas llamadas. Visita tres casas de muñecas. Vende cuatro bolsas de gorritos para la fiesta y se hace ochenta dólares. Llega a casa de Ivanka algo exhausta.

–Toma, guárdame cuarenta. Con los ciento sesenta que ya me tienes tengo doscientos, con trescientos más ya puedo rentar un cuarto.

–Así tienes que pensar, Charlotte. Una vez que tengas el cuarto te pones a pensar en novios.

–Sí, es verdad.

Charlotte se relaja en el sofá.

–Voy a descansar un rato, que esta noche tengo barra.

Se queda así, boca arriba pensando en el polaco, en lo que le ha dicho Ivanka, en los quinientos dólares

Manhattan, where they are right now. With five hundred she could pay for a whole month. But no. She's spent that much and a lot more on drugs.

«That's life, 007.»

The dog raises its head, looks at her.

Charlotte goes back to Ivanka's, leaves 007 and goes to get condoms at community centers, HIV testing centers, and the Gay Center. She sells the bags of condoms for twenty dollars. She sells them on to the locas who meet clients at their houses and don't go out to the bars to make their money. They put ads in the papers and on a website that's just appeared: Transsexual Escort Services. She makes a few calls. She visits three dollhouses. She sells four bags of condoms for the party, and makes eighty dollars. When she gets to Ivanka's place she's pretty exhausted.

«Here, keep forty for me. With the hundred sixty that you're already keeping for me, I have two hundred. With three hundred more I can get a room.»

«That's how you should be thinking, Charlotte. Once you have your room you can think about boyfriends.»

«Yeah, I know.»

Charlotte relaxes on the couch.

«I'm going to rest a while –– I've got the bar tonight.»

So she lays there, face up, thinking about the Polish guy, about what Ivanka told her, about the five

que necesita para rentar el cuarto y en todo lo que ha gastado en droga. Cuando de pronto suena el celular, ella sabe que es él.

–Yes, baby. How are you? Yes. So, you want to see me tonight. Yes. Nine pm is cool. Sure, babe. Aha. Aha. Aha. Then. Of course. How much you have for me. How. Much. You. Have. For. Me!

Recuerda que hay que pensar en el dinero, esa frase en la voz de Ivanka le da vueltas en la cabeza.

–Well, baby. I have to send money to my family too. I don't want go to the movies. I don't want you to take me to dinner. I don't want to be your girlfriend. I want money! No money, no honey! Good nite.

El 007 llega corriendo donde está Charlotte. Le ladra para despertarla del soponcio que le ha caído apenas cerró el celular. Charlotte se pone de pie como resorte y dice en voz alta:

–Sí, dinero es lo que necesito.

Y esa noche se va a trabajar.

En una semana reúne los quinientos dólares y se va uptown, a una agencia donde rentan cuartos. Consigue uno en la calle 143 y Broadway, donde una señora dominicana que tiene dos hijas rubias gordas y un esposo alcohólico. Ciento veinte dólares a la semana. Paga un mes completo.

Estaba siendo una semana muy ocupada.

Va a visitar a Vicky, su amiga ecuatoriana. Se le hace tarde. Ella le dice que se quede a dormir, que se tomen

hundred dollars she needs to rent the room, and about everything she's spent on drugs. When the cell rings all of a sudden, she knows it's him.

«Yes, baby. How are you? Yes, so you want to see me tonight. Yes. Nine pm is cool. Sure, babe. Aha. Aha. Aha. Then. Of course. How much you have for me. How. Much. You. Have. For. Me!»

She remembers she has to think about the money. That sentence of Ivanka's is running around in her head.

«Well, baby. I have to send money to my family, too. I don't want to go to the movies. I don't want you to take me to dinner. I don't want to be your girlfriend. I want money! No money, no honey! Good night.»

007 runs over to Charlotte. He barks at her to wake her up from the stupor she fell into as she closed her phone. Charlotte springs to her feet and says out loud, «Yes, money's what I need.»

So that night she goes off to work.

In one week she collects the five hundred dollars and goes uptown, to a room rental agency. She gets one on 143rd and Broadway, from a Dominican lady with two fat blonde daughters and alcoholic husband. One hundred twenty dollars a week. She pays for a full month.

It was getting to be a very busy week.

She goes to visit Vicky, her Ecuadorian friend. It's getting late. She tells her she can stay over –– they can

una botellita de ron y que se pongan a platicar. Charlotte propone que ella compre la bolsita de coca.

–¿Tienes algún contacto aquí en Brooklyn?

–Por supuesto, me ofendes –le responde Vicky.

Y así se la pasan, bebiendo y jalando. Charlotte se acuerda del polaco. Se acuerda de que nunca le ha preguntado su nombre. Se acuerda de lo guapo que es, a pesar que tiene una verga con mucho pellejo. Se acuerda de lo mal que lo trató en la última llamada. De que ahora ya tiene su cuarto y que se encuentra más relajada. Y además en ese momento está en Brooklyn, donde él vive. Seguro que en Brighton Beach, no muy lejos de allí. Se acuerda de que tiene guardado el teléfono en el celular. Se toma otro trago para darse valor. Su amiga Vicky, ni en cuenta; cuando se embala le da por leerse el tarot. Charlotte se pone de pie, va al cuarto de Vicky para estar a solas. Y ahí es bien confortable, parece el dormitorio de una casa antigua, pues Vicky gasta parte de su dinero en objetos buscados en los lugares más raros de New York City. Charlotte se recuesta en la cama con columnas, rodeada de cortinas, y marca el número del polaco.

–Aló. Aló. It's me. You remember me? Yes, Charlotte. You remember me? I'm in Brooklyn. You want to see me. No. No. Don't worry, I don't want money. I just want to tell you that you can come over. Yes. Yes. Call me back if you want. Okay. Okay. Bye.

drink a bottle of rum and just talk. Charlotte tells her she should buy a bag of coke. «Do you have any contacts here in Brooklyn?»

«Of course. Who do you think I am,» Vicky replies.

So they spend the whole night like this, drinking and snorting. Charlotte remembers the Polish guy. She remembers that she's never asked him his name. She remembers how handsome he is, in spite of the fact that he has a lot of foreskin. She remembers how badly she treated him on that last phone call. How she has her own room now and she's more relaxed. Plus right now she's in Brooklyn, where he lives. He probably lives in Brighton Beach, not very far from there. She remembers she has his number saved in her phone. She takes another drink to work up her courage. Her friend Vicky is clueless to all this; when she gets high she likes to read her tarot cards. Charlotte stands up and goes to Vicky's room to be alone. It's really comfortable in there –– looks like a bedroom in an old house, because Vicky spends part of her money on these little objects she finds in the strangest spots in New York City. Charlottes lies down on the poster bed surrounded by curtains, and dials the Polish guy's number.

«Aló. Aló. It's me. You remember me? Yes, Charlotte. You remember me? I'm in Brooklyn. You want to see me. No. No. Don't worry, I don't want money. I just want to tell you that you can come over. Yes. Yes. Call me back if you want. Okay. Okay. Bye.»

Charlotte se queda ahí, mirando el techo. Sabe que él no la va a llamar. Se pone de pie. Se dice en voz alta:

–Lo que necesito es dinero.

Camina hacia la cocina.

–Vicky, llama al delivery. Quiero otra bolsa de coca.

Charlotte lies there looking up at the ceiling. She knows that he is not going to call her back. She stands up. She tell herself, out loud, «What I need is money.»

She walks towards the kitchen.

«Vicky, call for a delivery. I want another bag of coke.»

Estas son nuestras banderas

Es domingo. Es el último domingo de junio. Me levanto de un salto de la cama. He dormido solo tres horas, pero igual me siento bien. Todo se siente muy buena onda. Igual anoche me hice mis chavos. Me voy corriendo al baño para darme una ducha. Me detengo. Me acuerdo de que tengo que llamar a la Myriam Hernández. La llamo. Creo que no va a contestar, su teléfono siempre está en vibrador. Pero no. No sé cómo ella lo escucha. La despierto.

–Que pasó –dice ella al otro lado del teléfono.

–¡Cómo que qué pasó! Levántate que hay que desfilar. ¡A ponerse bella! –le digo en la más rise and shine. Finalmente me voy al baño. A pesar de que hace unas cuantas horas me he afeitado, voy y me rasuro de nuevo. Tengo que estar perfecta. Es sólo una vez al año que salgo de día como toda una mujer. Bueno, sin contar las veces en que he sido arrestada y me dejan salir al otro día, a las diez de la mañana o a las tres de la tarde. Me doy una ducha que empieza tibia y termina fría. Me paso el chorro de agua por la espalda, es como una

These Are Our Flags

It's Sunday. It's the last Sunday in June. I jump out of bed. I've slept just three hours, but I feel good anyway. Everything feels cool, muy buena onda. I already made plenty of coins last night. I run to the bathroom to take a shower. I stop midway. I remember that I have to call Myriam Hernández. I call her. I think she's not going to answer, her phone is always set on vibrate. But no. I don't know how she hears it. I wake her up.

«What happened?» she says on the other end of the line.

«What do you mean 'what happened'?» Get up –– we have to go march. It's time to get dolled up!» I tell her in my best rise-and-shine. Finally I get to the bathroom. Despite the fact that I shaved only a few hours ago, I go and shave again. I have to be perfectly beautiful. It's only once a year that I go out in the daytime completely as a woman. Well, not counting the times I have been arrested and they let me out the next day, at ten in the morning or three in the afternoon. I take a shower that starts out lukewarm and ends cold. I pass the spray over my back,

inyección de energía. Me seco con una toalla limpia y blanca. Vuelvo a mi cuarto y pongo un CD de Pet Shop Boys. Any song is good. Me echo crema por todo el cuerpo. Busco un maletín de día. Lo lleno de todo lo necesario. Peluca, vestido, high hills, aretes, make up. Everything. Me miro en el espejo. Poso de una forma y otra. Agarro la bandera que voy a llevar al parade. Poso. Poso de nuevo. El espejo está enmarcado de fotos mías figurando con mis amigas. Me acerco y observo una en que estoy con la Myriam Hernández celebrando su cumpleaños. Pero of course: ella no es la cantante, sino su admiradora. Se ha ido haciendo cirugías plásticas para parecerse a ella. Y sí, después de tantas operaciones en realidad se parece a la de «El hombre que yo amo». Una de esas tantas cirugías la puso en tremendo aprieto hace un año atrás. Ella, bien divina, ya casi era igualita a la Myriam Hernández. Sólo le faltaban los ojos: tenía que achinárselos. Como es residente no tenía problema en salir y volver a Estados Unidos, así que decide irse a Ecuador, donde las operaciones le salían más baratas. Igual antes había ido a ese país a ponerse los pechos; era un paquete que incluía pasaje, cirugía, estadía y recuperación. Me acuerdo de que la acompañamos un grupo de locas al aeropuerto.

–Volveré para que me respeten –nos dijo antes de tomar el avión a Sudamérica.

like an injection of energy. I dry off with a clean white towel. I go back to my room and put on a Pet Shop Boys CD. Any song is good. I rub cream all over my body. I look for a rollerbag fit for daytime. I fill it with all the necessary items. Wig, dress, tacones, earrings, make-up. Todo. I look at myself in the mirror. I pose this way and that. I grab the flag that I'm going to take to the parade. I pose. I pose again. The mirror is framed by photos of me and my friends. I get close and see one of me with Myriam Hernández celebrating her birthday. Though of course you know: this is not the singer, but her admirer. She's been getting plastic surgery to look more and more like her. And so yes, after many many operations she really does look like the singer of «El hombre que yo amo.» One of those surgeries put her in a real bind a year ago. She was already fabulous, almost identical to Myriam Hernández. She was just missing the eyes: she had to get them narrowed. Being a resident she had no problem leaving the US and getting back in, so she decides to go to Ecuador, where the operations were cheaper. Besides, she had already gone there to get her chest done; it was a package that included travel, surgery, stay, and recovery. I remember a bunch of us locas went with her to the airport.

«I'll come back and I'll finally get some respect,» she told us before taking the plane to South America.

Y nosotras diciéndole que se iba a botar, que buena suerte. Otra loca le pedía que le trajera coca, porque dicen que la de allá es muy buena. Es la coca original. Otra loca cínica exclamaba que la iba a extrañar. Y calabaza calabaza, cada una para su casa. Myriam nos había dicho que volvería en una semana. Pasó la semana y no sabíamos nada de ella. Una loca que ya no era loca, sino que ya se había hecho el cambio de sexo, llegó a la barra y nos contó que a Myriam la habían deportado. Seguro que le habían cachado el record en el aeropuerto y, con la cantidad de arrestos por prostitución, demás que la mandaron de vuelta a su país de origen, El Salvador.

No había pasado ni un año desde que habían derribado las Torres Gemelas, y las cosas para cualquiera que fuera inmigrante se habían puesto difíciles, incluso si eras residente. La loca que ya no era loca hizo una especie de colecta para enviarle dinero. Cada una dio lo que pudo. La que decía que la iba extrañar no dio nada. Que no era su business, dijo.

Al mes y medio aparece Myriam, un viernes por la noche, en la barra.

–¡Loca, estás de vuelta! –le digo feliz y muy sorprendida.

–Ay, sí. Esa cruzada por México fue un infierno, así que esta noche vine a trabajar full. Mira que estoy quebradísima –me dice antes de irse.

146

We were all there telling her she was really going all the way this time, and good luck. Another loca asked her to bring her back some coke, because they say it's so good there. It's the original coke. Another loca shouted sarcastically that she was going to miss her. Then ladybug ladybug we flew away home. Myriam had told us that she would be back in a week. A week went by and we didn't hear anything from her. A loca who was no longer a loca because she had had a sex change, came to the bar and told us that Myriam had gotten deported. I guess they got a load of her record at the airport, and with that many arrests for prostitution, they went ahead and sent her back to the country of her birth, El Salvador.

It had not even been a year since the Twin Towers came down, and for any immigrant things had gotten difficult, even if you were a resident. The loca who was no longer a loca got together a kind of collection to send her money. We all put in what we could. The one who said she would miss her put in nothing. It was none of her business, she said.

A month and a half later Myriam showed up, one Friday night, at the bar.

«Loca, you're back!» I tell her, happy and very surprised.

«Ay, sí. Crossing through Mexico was a nightmare, so tonight I came to work like hell. I am flat broke,» she tells me before leaving.

147

Esa noche la vi salir y entrar unas cuantas veces.

–Llevo mil. Quiero otros más –me decía con una amplia sonrisa. Y sí, se los hizo. Ahora con los ojos achinados sí que era la gemela de Myriam Hernández.

Me doy cuenta de que el tiempo está pasando rápido. La llamo de nuevo. En una de esas se ha quedado dormida.

–Ya me duché –me dice.

–No te olvides de la bandera. Nos encontramos en la calle 39 entre la Quinta y la Sexta. En una hora. Sé exacta, marica –le digo antes de cortar.

Beso el rosario y le digo a la Virgen que se lo rezo cuando vuelva a la noche. Voy de afán. Salgo a la calle. Tomo el tren A, downtown. No espero por mucho tiempo. Me subo al tren y me siento mirando hacia afuera. La Myriam Hernández está de lo más feliz con poder desfilar en este parade.

–Pensé que no iba a estar aquí –me había dicho un par de noches atrás.

Así, vendada y todo, la habían puesto en un avión con destino a El Salvador. Y como ella tiene a toda su familia acá, pues estaba completamente sola. Pero es una chica dura de roer. En la estación de la calle 125 se suben dos morenas, cada una con la bandera del arcoíris. Van tomadas de las manos, una bien masculina y la otra bien femenina. Antes de que se cierren las puertas

That night I saw her leave and come back in several times.

«I have one thousand so far. I want a couple more,» she told me with a full smile. Yes, she had had them done. Now with her narrow eyes she really was Myriam Hernández's twin sister.

I see that time is going by quickly. I call her again. Maybe she's fallen back asleep.

«I already showered!» She tells me.

«Don't forget the flag. We'll meet on 39th between Fifth and Sixth. In one hour. Be on time, marica,» I tell her before I hang up. I kiss my beads and tell the Virgin I will pray the rosary when I get back tonight. I'm too eager to get out onto the street. I take the A-train downtown. I don't have to wait for it that long. I get on the train and sit, looking out. La Myriam Hernández is just so happy to be able to march in this parade.

«I thought I wasn't going to be here,» she'd told me a few nights earlier.

They had put her on a plane, bandaged up and everything, back to El Salvador. And since she has her whole family here, there she was completely alone. But she's a hard girl to break. At the 125th St. station two black girls get on, each one with a rainbow flag. They're holding hands, one butch and the other fem. Before the doors close two locas get on. Just

del tren entran dos locas. Lo que faltaba. Seguro que son boricuas. Se paran en el medio y se ponen a voguear. Muchos de los que van en el tren las vitorean, algunos las acompañan con las palmas de las manos. Cómo no. Ahí somos casi todos familia. Sisters. Esa noche, cuando Myriam me contó su odisea, nos estábamos haciendo un cliente. Ella me había llamado antes:

–Vente al hotel, que estoy con un pargo de party –me dijo por teléfono, justo antes de llegar uptown.

Por suerte andaba con chavos esos días, así que le dije al taxista que se diera media vuelta:

–All the way downtown. Financial district.

Alguien con dinero, pensé. Y sí, el hotel era fabuloso. Pasé sin problemas directo del lobby al ascensor. Myriam me abre la puerta de la habitación con cara de business woman y me da trescientos dólares apenas entro. En la cama hay un hombre ya cuarentón vistiendo lingerie. Stockins y high hills.

–Date un pase –me dice la Myriam, mientras me pasa un billete de veinte dólares enrollado como un tubillo para aspirar la coca.

–Ven a la cama –me dice, en la onda «yo soy la boss»–. Deja que el tipo te la mame.

Me saco la verga y el cliente empieza a mamar. Dejo que se entretenga por unos cuantos minutos y luego hablo:

–Ya basta. Necesito un break.

what we needed. Boricuas, I bet. They get up and start voguing down the center of the car. A bunch of people on the train cheer them on, some of them are even clapping along. Why not. Here we're all like family. Sisters. The other night, when Myriam recounted her odyssey to me, we were with a client. She had called me earlier:

«Come down to the hotel –– I'm partying with a john,» she told me over the phone, just before I got back uptown. Luckily I had coins on me that day, so I just told the taxi driver to turn around. «All the way downtown. Financial District.»

Someone with money, I thought. And yes, the hotel was fabulous. I went through the lobby and on to the elevators without any problem. Myriam opens the door looking like a businesswoman and gives me three hundred dollars as soon as I come inside. On the bed there's a man in his forties wearing lingerie. Stockings and high heels.

«Do a line,» Myriam tells me, handing me a twenty-dollar bill rolled up like a straw to snort the coke with.

«Come to the bed,» she tells me, in a 'I'm the boss' sort of tone. «Let the guy suck you.»

I take my dick out and the client starts sucking. I let him go for a few minutes and then I speak. «Enough. I need a break.»

–Sí –dice la Myriam–. Vamos, papi. Córrete la paja mientras ves la porno –le ordena al pargo, en la onda «para que nos dejes tranquilas por un momento».

–Dale otro pase para que se ponga más loco –le digo, pensando en que también quiero uno.

Y el cliente se da un pase. Yo dos.

–Mira, ese es el bar.

Le estoy indicando el mini fridge del cuarto.

Nos miramos con complicidad. Ella se pone de pie. Se acerca a la cama donde está el pargo y, susurrando, le pregunta:

–¿Babe, quieres estar más tiempo con nosotras?

–Of course.

El tipo tiene voz de embalado.

–Then more money! –alega la Myriam, pasándole el pantalón que está en el suelo.

Yo, en tanto, me he ido directo al pequeño refrigerador que está lleno de botellas de diferentes licores. Vacío en dos vasos algunas botellitas de Absolut. Les agrego hielo y cranberry juice: uno para mí, el otro para la loquita. Al pargo le alcanzo una cerveza:

–Dale otro pase.

El cliente se da uno. Yo dos.

–Que se siga corriendo la paja –tranquiliza la Myriam, mientras se sienta a mi lado en un sofá azul.

–Salud –le digo mientras me pasa un billete de cien dólares.

«Yes,» says Myriam. «Come on, papi. Jerk off while you watch that porno,» she orders the john, as if to say 'and just leave us alone for a minute.'

«Give him another line to get him wound up even more,» I say, thinking that I want another one too.

So the client does a line. I do two.

«Look –– there's the bar.» I'm pointing to the minifridge in the room.

We exchange a knowing glance. She gets up. She goes over to the bed where the john is lying, and whispers to him, «Babe, do you want to be with us a little more?»

«Of course.»

I can hear the high in his voice.

«Then more money!» Myriam demands, handing him the pair of pants from off the floor.

Meanwhile, I have gone directly to the small refrigerator that's stocked with bottles full of different liquors. I pour some little bottles of Absolut into two glasses. I add ice and cranberry juice: one for me, the other for my loquita. I get a beer for the john. «Give him another line.»

The client does a line. I do two.

«Let him keep jerking off,» says Myriam, coming down a little, as she sits down next to me on a blue sofa.

«Salud,» I say, as she passes me a hundred-dollar bill.

Seguro que el tipo le dio más, pero es cliente suyo. Así que yo más que happy. Nos tomamos los tragos de una, preparo otros más. Nos quedamos en silencio. Sólo se escuchan los sonidos que hacen los actores de la película porno.

–Y pensar que en tres meses me puse de pie –me dice con orgullo.

–Sí, te botaste.

–Te juro que nunca había llorado tanto. Una vez, cuando era un niño en El Salvador, camino a la escuela nos paró la guerrilla. Yo no sabía qué pasaba, y me puse a llorar sin saber por qué lloraba.

Se queda pensativa.

–Date otro trago.

Toma su cóctel y continúa:

–Y la segunda vez que lloré tanto fue cuando me subieron al avión para deportarme. Los guardias de inmigración eran bien cafres. No me dejaron llevar ni siquiera mis pastillas para el dolor que me había dado el doctor en Ecuador. Y yo recién cirugiada. Porque no sólo me achiné los ojos, también me achiqué un poco más la nariz.

–Y ahora sí que te pareces a la Myriam Hernández.

–Of course.

El tren ya llega a la calle 59, Columbus Circle. Se sube bastante gente. Sólo quedan dos estaciones.

I'm sure the guy gave her more than that, but it's her client. So I was more than happy. We drink our cocktails down, I make two more. We sit there for a minute in silence. You can hear only the sounds of the actors in the porno movie.

«And to think that in three months I got back on my feet,» she says to me with pride.

«Yeah, you really went all out.»

«I swear I never cried as much as I did then. Once, when I was a little boy in El Salvador, on my way to school the guerrilla stopped us. I didn't know what was going on, and I started crying without knowing why I was crying.» She pauses, lost in thought.

«Take another sip.»

She sips from her drink and continues: «And the second time I cried that much was when they put me on the plane to deport me. The immigration police were total brutes. They didn't even let me take the pills the doctor had given me in Ecuador for the pain. And me with work just done. Because they didn't just narrow my eyes; they also made my nose a little smaller.»

«And now you do look like Myriam Hernández.»

«Claro.»

The train is already getting to 59th St., Columbus Circle. A lot of people get on. Only two more

155

Llegamos rápido a la 42, Times Square. El tren se llena. Todo el mundo anda con ánimo de fiesta.

–Ni que fueran todas locas –murmuro.

Y sonrío.

Tres días atrás la Myriam me había llamado para que fuera a limpiarle el departamento. Y yo, como no le hago asco al dinero y sé que me dará una buena propina, voy volando en la más asesora del hogar. Apenas llego me da una lista larguísima para ir de compras al supermercado.

–Oye loqui, pero para qué vas a comprar tanta comida si tú vives sola –comento con la lista en la mano.

Ella me mira, como diciendo ve y calla. Vuelvo con cuatro bolsas llenas de abarrotes. Mientras acomodo las cosas en el refrigerador y donde puedo, escucho a la Myriam que me habla desde el dormitorio.

–Cuando estaba deportada, sin ningún quinto en el bolsillo, me iba a los McDonalds de San Salvador a ver si alguien dejaba algunas papas fritas o algún resto de hamburguesa. Rara vez encontraba algo, pues no es como acá. Tú sabes que en nuestros países la gente se come todo lo que pide. Aquí dejan la mitad. Así que ahora quiero ver mi casa llena de comida.

–Bueno, loquita, deja que me lleve algo. Mira que tirar comida es pecado –respondo bien fresca,

stops left. We get to 42nd St. Times Square quickly. The train fills up. Everyone is in a party mood.

«A whole train full of locas wouldn't even make this much noise,» I mumble to myself.

And I smile.

Three days ago Myriam had called me to go over and clean her apartment. And since I never turn down money and I know she'll give me a good tip, I fly over to her as any good housekeeper would. As soon as I get there she gives me a huge grocery list.

«Oye, loqui, how are you going to need so much food if you live alone?» I ask with the list in my hand.

She gives me a look like just be quiet and go. I come back with bags full of groceries. As I put everything away in the refrigerator and wherever else I can find to put it, I listen to Myriam talking to me from inside the bedroom.

«When I was away, deported, I didn't have a dime in my pocket, so I went around to the different McDonalds of San Salvador to see if anyone left some fries or a bite of a hamburger. I hardly ever found anything; it's not like here. You know how where we're from, people eat everything they order. Here they leave half of it on the tray. That's why, now that I'm back, I want to see my house chock full of food.»

«Ok, loquita, but let me take some of it with me. You know throwing away food is a sin,» I answer, fresh

mientras dejo algunos chocolates y galletas en una bolsa aparte.

Finalmente el tren llega a la calle 34, Penn Station. Me bajo. Miro la hora en mi celular. Estoy con el tiempo justo. Subo a la calle. Camino un par de cuadras. Llego al building donde vive la Fabrizzio, un amigo argentino. Toco el timbre varias veces, seguro que aún duerme. Finalmente me abre. Subo a su departamento. Tiene cara de sueño y embale.

–Dale, cámbiate rápido que quiero seguir durmiendo. Tengo la media nota –me dice volviendo a su cama.

Ni se me ocurre preguntarle si va a la parada, sólo me cambio en el baño en un dos por tres. Vestido blanco, zapatos de plataforma plateados, peluca castaña corta, aretes chandelier también plateados. Pongo con mucho cuidado la bandera en una bolsa para que no se arrugue, además de una pequeña cartera con el celular, algunos chavos, polvo de maquillaje y un lápiz labial rojo.

–Ya me voy –le aviso a la Fabrizzio.

–Nos vemos más tarde. Y no te olvides de dejar la puerta cerrada – dice desde su dormitorio.

Bajo rápido las escaleras desde el cuarto piso. No tengo tiempo para estar esperando el ascensor. Quiero llegar ya a la calle 39. Llego corriendo. Me instalo al lado de la carroza de Translatinas. Me preguntan si no me voy a subir con ellas.

as you can be, leaving some chocolate and cookies for myself in a separate bag.

Finally the train gets to 34th St., Penn Station. I get off. I check the time on my phone. I'm running just on time. I come up to the street. I walk a few blocks. I get to the building where an Argentinian friend, la Fabrizzio, is living. I ring the bell several times. Must be still asleep. Finally she buzzes me in. I go up to her apartment. She looks sleepy and high.

«Come on in, get changed quick so I can go back to sleep. I'm still kind of tripping,» la Fabrizzio says, heading back to bed.

I don't even think to ask if she's going to the parade; I just change in the bathroom quick as I can. White dress, silver platform shoes, short brown wig, and chandelier earrings, also silver. I place the flag in a bag very carefully, so that it doesn't get wrinkled, along with a small purse with my cell, some money, powder, and red lipstick.

«I'm out,» I yell to la Fabrizzio.

«I'll see you later. And don't forget to lock the door on your way out,» she says from the bedroom.

I run down the stairs from the fourth floor. I don't have time to be waiting for the elevator. I want to get to 39th St. I run all the way there. I set myself next to the Translatinas float. They ask if I want to climb up with them.

–No. Me gusta caminar –les respondo, mientras saco la bandera con mucho cuidado de la bolsa plástica.

Se escucha el sonido de un silbato. El Gay Parade ha comenzado. Se escuchan aplausos y vítores que vienen de todos lados.

–¡Tanto maricón junto! –grita una loca a carcajadas.

Alzo la bandera blanco, azul y roja con la estrella. La bandera de mi país. Cuando voy caminando como por la segunda cuadra alguien me toca la espalda. Me doy la vuelta: es la Myriam Hernández. Va toda vestida de blanco, también con su bandera celeste y blanca en las manos.

–¡Vamos, Miss El Salvador! ¡Alce esa bandera!

Es un domingo luminoso. Caminamos una al lado de la otra con nuestras banderas en alto. Una brisa que nos da en el rostro se sube a nuestras banderas y hace que ondeen más alto. Me acuerdo de Chile. Me acuerdo de Santiago. A nuestro pasar, la Quinta Avenida se transforma en una ancha Alameda.

«No. I like to walk,» I answer, as I take the flag very carefully out of the bag.

A whistle blows. The Gay Parade has begun. You can hear applause and cheers from every direction.

«So many maricones in one place!» yells one of us locas, laughing.

I raise the white, blue, and red flag with the star. The flag of my country. As I'm walking down like, the second block someone taps me on the back. I turn around: it's Myriam Hernández. She's dressed all in white, also with her light blue and white flag in her hands.

«That's right, Miss El Salvador! Wave that flag!»

It's a bright sunny Sunday. We walk side by side with our flags held high. A breeze hits us head-on, rises up to our flags, and makes them flutter even higher. I remember Chile. I remember Santiago. As we walk along, Fifth Avenue slowly turns into one wide Alameda.

Translator's Note
Marc Brudzinski

Never, Ever Ever, Coming Down is the first collection of short stories written by Iván Monalisa Ojeda. The original Spanish-language collection, *La misma nota, forever*, was first published in Santiago de Chile in 2014. Ojeda was born in Llanquihue, in the south of Chile, in 1966. He studied Theater Arts at the Universidad de Chile, in Santiago, where he became part of a community of artists that included Pedro Lemebel, one of the most famous queer artists from Latin America. In 1996, Ojeda came to New York on an artistic grant. Once in New York, Ojeda made friends with Latina sex workers who were transvestites and transgender and transsexuals and who gave Ojeda the name Monalisa. Ojeda identifies readily as transgender but when given a chance to elaborate, identifies more as two-spirit or gender non-conforming. Ojeda moves back and forth between «Iván» and «Monalisa» and accepts the pronouns «he» and «she.» In this collection, we read stories inspired by the experiences

that Monalisa and her friends, co-workers, and neighbors had in New York, some before the gentrification that took off under the mayoralty of Giuliani. Ojeda has lived in New York since 1996 and this debut collection is informed by the experience of crossing between male and female, between Spanish and English, and between the New York of impending gentrification and the New York of nostalgia.

This side-by-side bilingual edition of the short stories gives the reader a unique chance to savor the inter-linguistic dynamics at play. The format allows bilingual readers to elaborate their own translations, if they so desire, and to enter into a critical dialogue with the translation on the right side of the page. Looking over from the «Spanish» original on the left to the «English» translation on the right, the reader can even compare the intercultural dynamics at work between the original and the translation against the intercultural dynamics already embedded in the original. In the interest of contributing to this critical dialogue between reader and author and translator, I would like to offer an account of some of the choices I made while translating these stories. It is my hope that this Translator's Note will also be of interest to a non-Spanish-speaking reader if it is able to communicate some of the aspects that are necessarily lost in translation.

The most immediate challenge to the translation was the author's use of code-switching, or the way she moved between Spanish and English. The main language of narration and dialogue is Spanish, but there are words, bits of dialogue, and groups of sentences in English. The movement between English and Spanish in the source text obeyed certain logics that were both socially representative and artistically idiosyncratic.

There is of course a sizable body of writing that gives literary expression to the coexistence of Spanish and English in many parts of the United States: texts that include English words within Spanish syntax, or vice versa. Here, Iván Monalisa Ojeda has written short stories in a Spanish that is at times very Chilean and at other times Caribbean or Nuyorican. At still other times, the prominent use of words and whole exchanges of dialogue in English would make the text difficult for a monolingual Spanish-speaker. For a bilingual reader of the original collection, the Chilean expressions remind us of the narrators' origins, the English words remind us how firmly the narrators have anchored themselves in their new life, and the words from Caribbean Spanish and Spanglish that the Chilean-born narrators live their new life among other immigrants. It is therefore possible to read the mingling of different dialects

and languages on these pages as a sort of linguistic palimpsest that reflects not only the narrators' move from Chile to New York, but also previous generations' migration to New York from Puerto Rico, the Dominican Republic, and Mexico.

For the translator, however, an awareness of this linguistic dynamic does not make it any easier to render the stories into English. In fact, it complicates the task. The challenge is, in some ways, to complete the narrators' biographical linguistic trajectory from Spanish to English by producing an English-dominant version of the stories. And whereas in the original stories, one of the functions of the English words is to signal that Spanish is somehow insufficient to render a life dealing with US institutions, or that one language is insufficient to render a bilingual life, when translation moves the text majoritarily into English we risk flattening a highly textured text, pounding the palimpsest into something too thin. In other words, even if we think of the English terms in the original stories as a foretaste of what an English-language version would sound like, the answer for a translator could not be to produce an English-only text.

And yet, how could I produce a translation that is as multilingual as the original? I could not, for example, produce some sort of linguistic mirror where all the narration in Spanish became English, and all

the English words that appear in the original turn into Spanish words in the translation. In the original stories, the English words and phrases and proverbs have the important function of showing how deeply the narrators have rooted themselves into a new bilingual life in New York. For example, in «The Siamese Cat,» the narrator proverbializes, in English, «The early bird gets the worm.» The function of this short departure into English is to say that he has to act fast if he wants to get enough clients to make a living. It underlines the professional competition between the sex workers and by extension their participation in the cut-throat economy of New York. If the narrator quotes from this proverb in English, the implication is that he learned it here and that it is appropriate for describing a mercenary reality from here. However, if I were to render such a proverb in Spanish (in the interest of reproducing the interlingual rhythm of the original), then the implication would be wholly different, maybe even counter to the original. If the English-language narrator were to say «Al que madruga Dios lo ayuda» (the equivalent proverb in Spanish equivalent to «The early bird gets the worm»), the implication would be that he was drawing on folk wisdom learned during a childhood in Chile, possibly from an older family member, to strategize in this new context of sex work in New York. Of course,

now that I write that all down, I have to admit that that would also be an interesting intercultural dynamic. But it would mean losing the proverbial phallic image of the worm, replaced by an invocation of God. And it would mean losing a demonstration of the acquisition of a new cultural tradition in favor of the triumph of folk wisdom from home. And in that way, moreover, it would not respect the thrust of this narrator's self-characterization throughout the story as someone who savvily navigates this new economy on its own terms.

The same holds true at a larger level across the stories, where English tends to be used more heavily in certain circumstances. For example, Ojeda's narrators use English words to name institutions or social realities encountered in daily life in New York («SSI,» «front desk,» «pick-up bar»). The narrators also use English words in ways that are common to hear among people speaking Spanish in places like New York: «Anyway,» «nice,» «Oh my God.» At other times, English words pop up when the characters are talking about dressing up («make-up,» «high heels»), sassing each other («oh please»), or invoking the mercenary values needed to make a living in a competitive trade in a competitive city («vampire,» «then more money!»). One last category, however, has less to do with the lexical category and more to

do with the poetic effect achieved by switching languages mid-sentence. This is the case with the title, which I discuss below. In all these cases, care needed to be taken in deciding where Spanish words would be used in the translation so that they could produce an analogous effect. If I were to just include Spanish phrases in the translated stories according to some sort of mirroring logic, the effect would be opposite: instead of indexing how much the narrators had changed in adapting to New York, the insistent presence of Spanish would imply that they still needed to draw on their first language, perhaps even implying that their English resources were not sufficient to draw on.

It is important to keep in mind as well that the original collection also makes an intervention into a certain literary scene in Chile, an intervention for which it has garnered attention from the Chilean press. Most notably, the author was interviewed for *The Clinic*, the satyrical newspaper with a considerable circulation in the country. By focussing on transvestite and transsexual sex work and drug use, the original stories tell a certain tale to Chilean readers about the glamours and dangers of life in New York that contradicts prevailing narratives written by economically priviledged Chileans. The use of English words, and the kind of English words used,

help distinguish this collection from the other Chilean narratives about New York. By periodically foregrounding the narrators' Chilean origins, the original stories also make an intervention in the body of writing produced by Latin American immigrants, since in this corpus Chileans do not have as much visibility as Caribbeans or Mexicans. In the midst of all this, the first audience of these stories remains the community of people the characters are based on, who speak in a mix of languages and dialects similar to the one used in the narration. But an English-language version of the stories necessarily intervenes in a different cultural conversation. It is a story of queer lives in New York that are lived in large part in Spanish. It is also in its own way an immigrant's story. In the context of immigrants' stories in the US, the inclusion of non-English words runs the risk of being simply «colorful» or «cute,» an evocation of difference that fetishizes it instead of provoking thought.

For all these reasons, a strategy of compensation was in order: instead of making the stories multilingual by using Spanish in the same circumstances described above, in this translation the preponderance of Spanish words are the terms for sexual identities, terms of address related to them, or other terms of endearment: loca, loquita, loqui, chula, chulita, chica, trasvesti, amorcito, novio. My hope was that these

words would contribute to the readers' ability to feel that they can hear the characters speaking. It helps in this respect that these are the terms that the real people on whom the characters are based may well use in Spanish even when they are speaking English. As terms of address they would use them in Spanish because the relationship with the person addressed is a relationship lived out in Spanish. And as a description of a socio-sexual role, these terms do not enjoy a one-to-one correspondence with English-language terms. As a term of address, «loca» is not exactly «girl» or «queen» because it can be both, and more. And the label «travesti» is not exactly «transvestite» because it is more commonly used than «transvestite» and covers more identitary ground. So to translate these terms completely into English would leave the text feeling somehow over-translated, beyond what is interculturally necessary or even appropriate. For the same reason that the original stories talk about the particular attractiveness of a man when he is described as «un truck driver» or «un construction worker» rather than «un camionero» or «un albañil,» the translation needs to talk about «a travesti.»

Another kind of code-switching question involved moving between different national dialects of Spanish. The original short stories make regular use of words whose national origins are recognizable

and mark different characters with an Argentinian, Dominican, or Puerto Rican nationality. I preferred to leave the marked words (e.g. «che,» «chelitos,» «boricua,» respectively) in Spanish, especially where the context would allow a non-Spanish-speaking reader to ascertain the part of speech without necessarily being able to guess the exact definition. In this way, hopefully these words could leave non-Spanish-speaking readers feeling at least a little out of their element, without constituting a stumbling block or breaking the flow of the rhythm. They could match the effect of the English words in the original.

The few uses of Spanglish terms (such as the description in «The Boy Next Door» of a locked bathroom door as «laqueada») were harder to duplicate. I translated them into informal English since the meaning would be relatively clear from context and leaving them in Spanglish would not push the reader into any more meaningful question. Also, since it would stand out in English more than «laqueada» stands out in Spanish, and since the switch would appear syntactically unmotivated, it seemed that such a use of Spanglish in the translation would contribute more to the fetishization of difference rather than stimulating intercultural curiosity.

Another challenge inherent in the prospect of translating this text was what to do with the way it

plays between different genders. Characters may describe themselves using feminine adjectives in one sentence and masculine adjectives further on. This feature is as noticeable in the original text as the code-switching is, but it is not as widespread; every story uses code-switching but not every story plays with the linguistic markers of gender. The gender-switching is possible in Spanish because all adjectives need to be marked for gender; in many cases, this means marking masculine adjectives with a final «-o» and feminine adjectives with an «-a.» Theoretically, the fact that Spanish adjectives need to be marked for gender allows Ojeda to call attention to a a linguistic transgendering without calling attention to the fact that a given adjective has any gender to begin with. In English the situation is different since there is not a simple morphological way to mark gender except with third-person pronouns. So I could use «he» and «she» to mark shifts in characters other than the narrator. But when narrators want to mark a shift in gender in the first person, they need to mark the presence of a gender, thereby calling more attention to the gender than was the case in the original. Since the gender-shifts needed to be noticeable without calling inordinate attention to themselves, I tried to reproduce the occasional adjectival shift in gender feature by selecting adjectives that are coded feminine, such

as when I translated «Tengo que estar perfecta» as «I have to be perfectly beautiful» or by using ways of speaking that are conventionally coded as feminine, such as when I translated «Estoy cansada» as «I'm just so, so tired.» There was one more way of mainting the gender play, which was easier: when characters are referred to by their first name preceded by the definite article. Thus, we have «la Manuel» and «la Fernando.» The wager is that U.S. readers, even if they do not speak Spanish, will notice the use of a feminine article in front of a masculine name. As it happens, this use of the definite article when mentioning a person's name is very common in Chilean Spanish, so there were many opportunities to take advantage of this in the translation.

My conversations with Ojeda, more than being endlessly entertaining and gratifying, were enormously helpful to me in understanding the tone I would want to shoot for. I wanted to keep the dramatic switches of rhythm, the dry and almost acerbic sense of humor, and the playful slipping across genders and across languages that leave the reader smiling in the air somewhere in-between. So that the reader could feel a kind of a high, as Ojeda suggested. I wanted to keep the reader as entertained as anyone who is reading or listening to Iván Monalisa in Spanish. Occasionally, this meant playing with the dramatic or comic

rhythm of the English sentence for the sake of reproducing an effect for the reader while using different
tools. This was possible in places where the rhythm
could compensate for other tools that the author had
at her disposal, such as the play between genders and
languages. This was a particular challenge with the
title of this collection, which is taken from a conversation between two characters in the story of the same
title. In this conversation the narrator is marvelling at
the life of an older friend she is talking with, a friend
who has kept the same attitude about life despite the
fact that she doesn't do drugs anymore. The narrator
tells this friend, «Anyway, como que tú te quedaste
en la misma nota forever.» The «nota» is a metaphor
that recurs throughout the collection and it refers to a
high, like the kind you experience on a drug. It's a figure so common that it doesn't stand out as metaphor
in everyday language, but the narrators play with its
metaphoricity on different occasions. I wanted to call
on the «high» metaphor in English, because it's ana-
logously unremarkable. But the end of the sentence
uses the English word «forever.» The jump to English
reproduces the feel of Spanish spoken in New York,
but it also has a rhetorical function beyond its definition. When I imagine the line being spoken, I hear the
word «forever» pronounced slightly elongated to hold
the marvel. The switch lifts you a little off balance, and

the length of the word keeps you suspended there. I tried to approximate that feeling by elongating the first part of the sentence and by adding the superfluous but quasi-lyrical «ever ever.» It doesn't duplicate all the magic of the original sentence, but I hope it compensates for this by echoing or foreshadowing the deferral of the older friend's final descent to the shelf behind the ending curtain waiting for her downstairs.

In this translation, the challenges posed by the mixing of languages and of genders reflect a larger question in translation studies. That question, posed by translators since Jerome, is whether it is better for translators to «domesticate» or «foreignize» the source text for the reader in the target language (to use terms prevalent in translation studies). That is, whether it is better for the translation to tame the foreignness in the source text in order to assimilate it to the reader's frame of reference, and in this way bring the source text into the world of the reader, or whether it is better to allow parts of the translation to remain conspicuously foreign, and in that way draw readers out of their world and into the world of the source text. My intent here was to foreignize the text for English-language readers, since the original stories already produce that effect for Spanish-language readers. The stories foreignize themselves by

crossing national languages from a perspective that is already widely transnational. They cross genders from a perspective that is already deeply transgender. We could even go so far as to claim that the original stories are already translations, in the sense that they are experiences that cross human categories. At the same time, when the narrators speak across linguistic categories, they do so in a way that anchors them in a specific social position. And in that social position, Spanish and English have different valences that a translation necessarily alters. The original stories are so compelling because the mix of languages and genders in them is not just a theoretical combination; its import is firmly grounded in a specific lived transcultural context. With such huge stakes I took comfort in George Steiner's reminder that when translators' failures have the benefit of drawing attention to «the resistant vitalities, the opaque centres of specific genius in the original.»* It is my hope that this translation does produce an initial estrangement for readers, and that this estrangement leads to curiosity and empathy. In the places it does not, my failure serves to highlight the uniquely estranging effects of the lives evoked in these stories.

*Steiner, Georges. «The Hermeneutic Motion.» in George Steiner, *After Babel: Aspects of Language and Translation*, Oxford: Oxford UP, 1975, pp. 296-303.

SANGRÍA

UNITED STATES PUBLICATIONS

Legibilities
1. *Art Cards / Fichas de arte*, Gordon Matta-Clark
2. *Never, Ever Ever, Coming Down,* Iván Monalisa Ojeda
3. *The Book of the Letter A*, Ángel Lozada
4. *They Have Fired Her Again*, Claudia Hernández

Radicalities
1. *Not in Our Name. Against the US Aid to the Massacre in Gaza /
Contra la ayuda de los Estados Unidos a la masacre de Gaza,*
various authors

PUBLICACIONES EN CHILE

Narrativas contemporáneas
1. *El arca (bestiario y ficciones de
treintaiún narradores hispanoamericanos),*
compilación de Cecilia Eudave y Salvador Luis
2. ~~*Los perplejos,* Cynthia Rimsky~~ [fuera de circulación]
3. *Segundos*, Mónica Ríos
4. *Caracteres blancos*, Carlos Labbé
5. *Carne y jacintos*, Antonio Gil
6. *La risa del payaso*, Luis Valenzuela Prado
7. *El hacedor de camas*, Alejandra Moffat
8. *Oceana*, Maori Pérez